THE POWER OF PERSUASION

THE POWER OF PERSUASION

THE TRIAD SERIES, BOOK 2

KATE PEARCE

1

ARCTIC REGION: 229990. NIMBUS SCIENCE STATION. EARTH.

"So, how can I help you, Doctor?"

Neeve stood to attention in front of the new base commander who sat behind his desk, his hands folded in front of him, his rather harsh face devoid of expression. Captain McNeill was a lot younger than the last man who'd held the job, and a lot harder to please. Since his arrival three months previously, he'd set the base on its ear reviewing everything from security details to the catering and lab schedules. No one had a good word to say about him, especially the scientists who hated having their little worlds disturbed.

"I wonder if you've had a chance to review my personal file, yet, sir?"

He raised one dark eyebrow. "I can't say that I have. There have been more pressing things to deal with than delving into the personal business of my subordinates." He glanced down at his tablet. "I do note, however, that you are a Pavlovan, and that you have been here for almost three years. What else do you think it is imperative for me to know?"

Her cheeks heated at his dry tone. Part of her wanted to walk away, but she didn't have that option.

"Pavlovan culture is based around the power of the number three."

He nodded. "So I understand."

"When I arrived here, my posting was for three Earth years, which will end shortly. I was originally sent here with my Second Male, but—"

"Hold up. Explain *second male*."

"As I said, our culture is based on the power of three. He was my mate."

"Why not first mate?"

"Because that was the designation he received when he visited the Oracle."

He looked at her as if he expected more information, but she remained resolutely silent. She would *not* discuss her loss with a man who probably had the sensitivity of the freezing arctic winds that circled the base like hungry predators.

"So what does the lack of a 'second male' have to do with your scientific research here?"

She stared resolutely at a dark spot on the wall past his right shoulder. "My mate was killed by suspected enemies of our planet shortly after we arrived here."

"It was a political murder?" His voice sharpened.

"It's all on file, sir." *Which, he should've read regardless of his so-called duties...*

"Do you think you are in danger?"

"Possibly, but that isn't the main problem. I'm coming to the end of a three year cycle, and my Second Male is dead." She cleared her throat. "I have certain... biological needs that were triggered by finding a mate."

"What kind of needs?"

"Sexual ones."

He leaned back in his chair and regarded her steadily. "What exactly does that entail? Do you go into a breeding cycle like the Kelevans?"

Neeve relaxed slightly. For the first time since he'd taken over the base, she was grateful for his cool, detached manner.

"If I had mates, it would certainly be the time to consider breeding. But in this instance, as I'm alone, it simply means my responses are heightened, and that I would be seeking out my sexual partners."

"Do you become a sexual predator?"

"Nothing quite so dramatic, sir. Everyone on the base is quite safe because none of you are Pavlovan. For three days in each Earth month for the next three months, I will need to be off duty and possibly sedated to control those natural impulses."

"And what if there's an emergency during the time you require off?"

She finally met his gaze and noticed that his eyes were a very dark blue that looked almost as black as his uniform. He was a hard male to fathom, this new commander of theirs. As a telepath she usually found human minds easy to read, but not this man's. He'd developed shields a Pavlovan would be proud of. She had no idea why.

"If I was sedated and the base was under attack, I would have to trust you to make a decision about whether to leave me behind or try and wake me up, sir. I understand that I might be a liability."

He regarded her steadily for a long moment and then nodded. "I appreciate you telling me this, Doctor. When do you anticipate needing the time off?"

"In the next week or so, sir."

"Then we'll work around you. I've been told to accommodate the needs of our Pavlovan guests very carefully indeed."

Neeve raised her chin. "I've never asked for special treatment before, Captain McNeill."

"I wasn't suggesting that you had." He rose to his feet signaling the audience was at an end. He was tall for a human, topping her by a head. "Thank you."

She saluted and walked out, slowly shutting the door behind her, and made her way back to the lab. *Heeze,* that had been embarrassing, but it would've been worse if she suddenly started losing focus during a mission and tried to screw someone. For the captain's benefit, she'd tried to minimize the effect the three days would have on her as she yearned for a mate who was no longer alive. It would be extremely difficult and emotionally devastating. She missed Malke like an amputated limb, but a human male like Captain McNeill, whose species was only just starting to develop telepathic links, wouldn't understand that.

Which was why she'd kept the information to the more practical and physical aspects of her needs. What was strange, and was something she'd decided to keep to herself was that after two years her urge to mate had suddenly returned with a vengeance. With almost no available partners on Earth, she'd assumed her instincts would remain dormant until she returned to Pavlovan and sought out the Oracle to find her another mate. But perhaps she had just been in mourning?

She wished she had someone to ask, but all her family were still on Pavlovan. It was ironic that she'd spent half her life wanting to get away from her home planet and now missed it more than she would ever have believed. Losing Malke had only made things worse, but she'd been determined to finish out her three-year stint and then go back. She had some pride...

She reached her lab and collapsed into her chair. At least that was over. Now all she had to do was focus on her work until the heat took her, and she could sleep the worst of her natural instincts away.

CAPTAIN IAN MCNEILL put down the file he'd been reading and rubbed his eyes. With the lack of natural light within the base, it was difficult to tell what time it was, but he sensed it was late. Dr. Neeve was a very interesting female with abilities Earth scientists were just starting to observe and recognize in the ever-evolving human population. It was a shame her mate had been killed. Despite her desire to keep things away from the personal, he'd sensed her deep grief for her male. She'd reminded him of how he'd felt about losing Leah...

He pushed the darkness away and concentrated on the present. For some reason, the government was on high alert about the latest feud between the Pavlovans and the Etruscans. All base commanders had been ordered to keep a close eye on their off-world personnel.

Not that he *had* many personnel. He could only surmise that he'd finally pissed off someone high enough in rank to get him sent on this shit poor assignment at the end of the frigging world. His particular skill set was hardly useful in a research center, and he certainly hadn't endeared himself to the scientists. But was there more to it than that? Dr. Neeve had mentioned her mate was murdered. Did the government think she needed special protection? Was that why he was there? If so, he wasn't sure if he appreciated becoming someone's bodyguard without being informed about it.

He opened a link to the central military operations room in London, and the disgruntled face of one of his only friends left in the military flashed up.

"What the hell, Mac? It's three o'clock in the morning."

"You're awake and at work, so what's the problem?"

"I was napping."

"Good to know that the security of our planet is in such safe hands."

"Sod off. What do you want?"

"Can you switch to privacy mode?"

"Sure." Dan's face wavered and then reappeared against a blue screen. "This better? Now what's up?"

"Do you know why they assigned me to Nimbus?"

Dan blinked. "Because the commander retired."

"And what else?"

"Oh that." Dan's grin widened. "It's kind of interesting, isn't it?"

"What is?"

"Oh shit, haven't they told you yet? Have you checked your security filters?"

"Just tell me."

"Okay, but promise me you'll check you have them set up right because I'm fairly certain you should have had this information." His smile faded. "You've got one of the Pavlovans up there, right?"

"Yes, a Dr. Neeve."

"You're supposed to be protecting her with your Extra Special Skills."

"I thought we weren't supposed to use them anymore."

"Yeah, well, the experiment is technically over, and the unit disbanded, but they can't change what they did, so they might as well make use of us." Dan scrubbed a hand over his face. "I don't like it any more than you do, but from what I hear you might be the key to her coming out of this latest inter-planetary conflict alive."

"It's that serious?"

"I don't know why this doctor is so important, but they send the best to look after her—you--so you'd better be prepared for anything."

"Fuck." Mac thought about his Pavlovan's impending mating crisis. "This really isn't a good time."

"It never is." Dan's gaze flicked to one side. "I gotta go."

"Thanks for the intel."

Dan's face faded and Mac stared at the blank blue screen.

"Well hell," he murmured. Fingers flying over the keyboard, he called up all seven of the different messaging systems on his tablet and finally located a file in his trash that looked like something his government would send. It took another five minutes to find the necessary security codes to open the fucker, but he managed it at last.

Security priority: Neeve, Doctor of Science. Pavlovan female. A++ class security required and authorized.

Ian read the remainder of the coded message. It was pretty straightforward. He was to guard the Pavlovan with his life from an undisclosed threat. He was cleared to use his augmented powers if necessary.

Now that was unheard of. Mac sat back. Neeve must be a very important person indeed if the military were prepared to use him to protect her. He reread her personal file and that of Malke, the male who had been killed, but there was no more information to be gleaned there. How the hell was he supposed to protect her if she was knocked out for three days? Was he expected to sit by her bed and hold her hand?

Not that it would be a hardship. She was a beautiful woman with pale skin long reddish hair and deep brown eyes. She spoke quietly, but there was an air of authority about her that made others listen. Her scientific research was considered groundbreaking and offered hope to millions of humans with defective gene alignments. Was that why the government really wanted to keep her alive—to benefit their own kind? He wouldn't put it past them.

And she would soon need sex…

Mac shut down the files and detached his mind from his tablet. Whatever the situation, he had the ability to keep her safe. After all, that was what he'd been trained for, not to run a research station in the freezing cold asscrack of the universe.

2

NEEVE FOCUSED ON PACKING THE ESSENTIALS FOR THE TRIP TO the outpost and tried to ignore her growing sense of unease. She felt *threatened*. She had a sense that if she approached Captain McNeill with her nebulous sense of dread, he wouldn't be impressed. He struck her as a hard man with little imagination. She also had no idea if the threat was mental or physical. If she was about to be attacked, she had the ability to defend herself. If it were a telepathic issue, she'd get no help from anyone at Nimbus anyway.

With a sigh, she straightened her back, picked up her bag and headed down to the vehicle bay. To her surprise, Captain McNeill was in there talking to one of the mechanics. He looked up as she approached.

"I'm coming with you. I haven't visited all the outposts yet. This seemed as good an opportunity as any."

"Yes, sir."

She busied herself loading her gear onto the All-Terrain Vehicle and checked her weapons. It wasn't her place to question command decisions, but she was grateful he was coming

9

along. She sensed that he would be a very good man to have beside her in a fight.

"What's the purpose of this trip?"

"I've been drilling down and taking samples of the ice pack to compare the atmosphere, pollution and indicators of life over the last few centuries."

"And what good does that do?"

"It gives me a baseline to compare how your species reacts to different climactic environments and how it has affected the current structure of your genes. If I can detect where the anomalies originated, I might be able to go back and find the correct gene sequences that preceded them and replicate them."

"Makes sense." He walked back over to his ATV and pulled up the hood of his thermal coat. "Are you ready to go?"

He was a man of few words. She nodded and mounted her vehicle, adding gloves and covering her head to counteract the below freezing temperatures outside. Despite the advance in lightweight fabrics to keep out the intense cold, it was still a dangerous environment for warm-blooded species. And with her telepathic senses all riled up, she sensed it could become even more dangerous than she could possibly imagine.

THEY REACHED the small outpost before it got too dark and put the ATV's in the heated garage area. Neeve led the way, snapping on the lights to reveal the sparse interior which consisted of two bedrooms, a central living area with a tiny kitchen and a large well-heated shower room.

"Nice." Captain McNeill commented as he dumped both their bags on the kitchen table.

"It's functional, sir. The lab is attached by a covered walkway through that door at the back." She pointed at the refrigerator and freezer. "There are enough rations in there to see us through any inclement weather patterns."

"Have you ever been stuck up here?"

"Only once, sir, but Malke was with me then, so we managed to keep each other amused until we were able to leave."

He gave her a sideways glance before picking up his bag and heading into the smaller of the two bedrooms. "How long do you imagine it will take to get your samples?"

"Less than twenty-four hours, sir. If I start this afternoon we'll be able to depart tomorrow night."

"Good. Let me know when you intend to set out."

She hesitated. "You don't have to come with me."

He looked at her over his shoulder. "What else do you expect me to do? Sit here and twiddle my thumbs?"

She had no answer to that, so she continued to her own room. When she emerged a few minutes later, he was in the kitchen stirring two mugs.

"Here you go."

"Thanks." She took the mug and studied the contents dubiously. "What is it supposed to be?"

"Vegetable and protein soup."

Neeve sipped at the thick liquid and repressed a shudder. Earth military rations were even worse than Pavlovan ones, and that was saying something.

"We can get suited up and go out after this. The sample sites are quite close."

"Good, because it's fucking freezing out there."

She found herself smiling. "You sound like Malke. He always hated the cold."

"You miss him, don't you?"

"He was my mate, physically, mentally and telepathically."

"That's a tough thing to lose." He finished his soup.

"Are you mated, sir?"

He stood up and shoved in his chair. "Not anymore."

"Your mate died?"

"Five years ago. Now shall we get on? I'd prefer to be back inside before it gets too dark."

Neeve stood too. "Yes, sir." She washed out her mug and headed back into her bedroom to get her snow gear, which took some wiggling into. It was made of a thin white fabric that covered her from head to toe like a second skin. The fabric responded to her body temperature, heating and cooling at will to provide her the best working environment possible. She'd often wondered how scientists functioned in the old days when they'd been bundled up in twenty layers of clothing.

As she pulled the hood over her braided hair she paused thinking about Captain McNeill's reaction to her questions, or, *more* importantly, his lack of reaction. He'd given away nothing, not a hint of emotion, or pain, or grief for his mate, which for a human was quite extraordinary. Either he was a very cold man, or he had the ability to shield his emotions like a Pavlovan.

Neeve finished dressing and walked across to the lab to pick up her prepared pack. Captain McNeill was waiting for her in the well-lit garage. He wore a matching white snowsuit that only emphasized his well-toned torso and muscular arms and legs. He looked like a man who should be scaling mountains or saving the world, not babysitting her at a research center.

"Do we need to drive?" he asked.

"Yes, it's only a couple of kilometers, but the weather can change very quickly. I don't want to risk being stranded and disoriented."

"Then shall we take one vehicle?"

"Sure. The coordinates are already set. Just turn the navigation system on and it should be the first destination listed."

He started up the ATV and she stowed her pack and then hopped on behind him wrapping her arms around his waist. He was surprisingly warm and she rubbed her cheek against his back like a *feerkit*.

"Ready?"

"Yes, sir."

She should sit back, but after almost two years on her own, she found she didn't want to relinquish a centimeter of his warmth. He didn't seem to mind her embrace so she inched even closer and felt a corresponding heat build low in her stomach. The growl of the ATV engine echoed her purr of satisfaction as the engine vibrated through her, making the ride rather more stimulating than she had anticipated.

When they reached their destination, she hopped off as fast as she could and set about unloading her gear. She could only hope her physical reaction to him was an aberration because of her approaching mating heat. Thank the Gods; she'd not felt any direct response from Captain McNeill. Luckily, he wasn't paying her much attention, his gaze on the white blur of the horizon, his weapon already out. She concentrated on extracting the ice probe from its icy sheath and soon forgot everything, but what she was doing.

MAC CIRCLED around the small site with a growing sense of unease. Something was out there, and it wasn't showing up on any scans. He just knew it was there and that it was a threat. He glanced back at Dr. Neeve and found her watching him, her expression wary.

"What is it?" She slowly rose to her feet and scanned the horizon. "What's wrong?"

"You sense it too?" Mac walked over to her. "Can you pick up anything telepathically?"

"Only—"

"Get down." Something caught the edge of his vision and he looped an arm around her and lunged toward the cover of the nearest snowdrift, his body covering hers completely. He lowered his head as a ball of fire burst over them and the ATV exploded, raining bits of hot metal and fuel down over him. Another roar and they were completely covered in snow.

He heard the crackle and pop of advancing gunfire and lay as still as he could using the limited oxygen around their heads as sparingly as possible. He didn't recognize the language the attackers were using. It didn't make any difference. They were here to kill. His job was to make sure they didn't succeed.

Beneath him Dr. Neeve wiggled and he increased the pressure of his body over hers holding her in place. She moved again and he set his teeth on her earlobe.

"No. Keep still."

At his direct telepathic command she went quiet and he eased some of his weight off her. Thank God for the white snowsuits that made them blend so effortlessly into their surroundings. Gunfire raked over the research site and then all went silent. He used all his senses to scan the area and slowly counted off the minutes. There were very few options open to them. They stayed where they were and froze to death. They moved and were shot dead by one of the remaining ambushers. Personally he preferred the second worst-case scenario. At least he'd have a chance at getting to the attacker and give Dr. Neeve an opportunity to escape.

He slowly inhaled and picked up the buttery scent of the doctor's soap and a hint of warmth that made him want to burrow his face against her neck and bite her again. At the moment, neither of them were cold thanks to their suits, but that would change. She slowly rolled her hips and her ass slid over his cock making him want to groan. It was definitely not the time to be thinking about how good it felt to have a female underneath him. One who was warm and pliant and *rubbing herself against him like a cat...*

Very slowly he planted one of his hands down beside her shoulder and tried to ease away from her, but she simply followed, filling the space, making his stupid cock far too aware of the sweetness of her flesh. His other arm was wrapped around her chest and now he could distinctly feel the hard thrust of her nipples against his covered skin.

"We're going to have to move in a second. Be ready to run when I give you the word."

She didn't say anything but her body tensed for action.

"Go."

He rolled off her in a blur of motion and came to his feet, his weapon at the ready. A faint shadow to his left had him firing off several rounds one handed. He registered a squawk of pain and the thud of something dropping to the ground. He hauled the doctor up and, keeping a hand wrapped around her arm, ran away from the still burning ATV and toward the nearest solid object they could hide behind.

With the wall at his back, he pulled her down beside him and pressed his mouth to her ear.

"Did you recognize the language?"

"Etruscan." She barely made a sound either.

"They'll probably wait for us back at the base, so let's go."

"Back *there*?"

"There's nowhere else *for* us to go. We'll die out here if we don't find shelter." He tapped the transmitter on his shoulder. "No signal either. Is there an emergency beacon at the post?"

"Yes, two. One in the lab, one in the living quarters."

He nodded and stared out into the rapidly darkening landscape using his enhanced senses array to plot the quickest course back to the base.

"Come on."

"Wait." She grabbed his sleeve. "Why didn't you tell me that you're telepathic?"

"It's a long story." He patted her arm. "Let's move it out."

NEEVE WASN'T sure which was more frustrating, Captain McNeill insisting they head right back into danger, or him refusing to discuss the fact that he'd spoken to her telepathically at least twice. She supposed the possibility of being killed outweighed everything else, but it was infuriating. And just to add to the stupidity of the situation, he'd stretched himself over her like a blanket and now all she could think about was how he'd felt, his smell, his weight on her, and the press of his cock against her ass.

She stumbled and he instantly stepped in and set her upright. His grip was like iron, just like the press of his cock… Gods this was ridiculous. She kept moving, aware that time was against them and that even the miraculous fabric of their clothing couldn't keep them warm forever. It seemed to take ten times longer to cover the short distance than she'd estimated. Ahead of her, Captain McNeill stopped and touched her shoulder.

"We're almost there. Are you okay?"

She narrowed her gaze. In the distance, she could see the faint lights of the research post. He obviously had excellent night vision.

"I'll find you a safe place to hide and I'll take these bastards out and come back."

She wrapped a hand around his bicep. "Hang on. You have no idea how many of them there are, and I'm not going to be stashed away like a parcel while you get yourself out-numbered and killed. I can fight. I've received military training."

His smile was lethal, his blue eyes like lasers against the whiteness of the snow. "Not like mine. I'm trained for exactly these types of situations."

She raised her chin and repeated. "I'm not going to be left behind."

"Dammit." He sighed. "Where's your weapon?"

She produced it and he nodded. "Okay, you can take the

back entrance of the lab. If anyone comes out of there, or at you from any side, you shoot them."

"Dead?"

"I'd highly recommend it."

He started walking again in a more circuitous pattern. Before he shut her out again, a sense of his complex and murderous thought processes suddenly slammed into her. Gods, his thought waves were like nothing she'd ever encountered before. It was like eavesdropping on a telepathic machine.

She followed him closely until he brought them up at the back of the lab building. The security systems around the post were obviously down. He indicated one of the walls that hid the trash disposal units.

"Wait here, put your back against the wall. You've got a clear view of the lab door, and no one can come up behind you without you hearing them."

Even his voice sounded less human. What the hell was he? He turned away and she caught his sleeve.

"Be careful."

He nodded and was gone so swiftly that by the time she blinked he was nowhere in sight. She leaned against the wall and assumed her firing stance, her gaze fixed firmly on the door.

The noise started quietly, a low rumble that built as something shrieked and then three single gunshots that reverberated in the chilling night air. She refocused her aim on the back door breathing out slowly the way she'd been taught. A shadow flitted by one of the windows and she stiffened as a faint telepathic probe touched her mind.

She knew there were some telepaths in the Etruscan army. Was that how they'd found her? If so, they now knew she was still alive. She focused on her shields, shutting herself down at much as possible, her gaze never leaving the back of the lab. A figure launched itself out of the door straight for her. She raised her weapon eased down on the trigger and fired.

The female stumbled, but kept coming, her red blood now staining the snow, her arm reached out to grab hold of Neeve. Bracing herself against the wall, Neeve kicked out at her assailant, knocking them both back on the snow and then she fired again. This time into the back of her assailant's skull. Inside her head, the telepath screamed and Neeve screamed right along with her.

Then all went quiet. Nothing moved anymore and the snow around her just kept getting redder. Neeve tried to breathe through her clenched teeth and heard a wispy whistling sound that surely didn't come from her.

"Doc, I'm behind you. Don't shoot."

She stayed still but she didn't lower her weapon until he came out in full sight, hands raised. He stared down at the figure sprawled in the snow.

"Nice job."

Her hands were shaking so badly that she almost couldn't lock her weapon. He waited while she completed the task, his gaze everywhere, and his stance predatory.

"There were four of them. I got the other three." He held out his hand. "It's safe to come back in now. I've already contacted base, and they'll be sending an armed unit up here as soon as the storm blows over."

Neeve finally holstered her weapon and stood. Her knees gave way and she slid down the wall again. McNeill was on her in a flash and crouched in front of her.

"Are you hurt?"

She shook her head and stared into his calm indigo eyes. They reminded her of the night sky.

He touched her arm. "Doc?"

"I killed her."

With a shudder, she threw herself at him and buried her face in his shoulder. After a second, his arms came around her and he held her tight.

"You did what you had to do. We're going to be fine."

She was shaking too hard to care what he was saying, and too intent on keeping him chained to her to do anything but breathe in the smell of death, discharged weapons and him... Gods. He smelled wonderful. She rubbed her lips over his throat, nuzzling at the fabric there.

"Doc..."

She looked at his mouth and licked her lips before leaning in and claiming the kiss she'd been wanting ever since he'd landed on top of her in the snow. His lips were cold, but he parted them without hesitation and let her questing tongue inside the volcanic heat of his mouth. His hands shifted on her body drawing her close until she was pressed against him from head to groin.

"You're in shock," he whispered against her lips. "This is just a surfeit of adrenalin. You need to get inside and lie down."

"Only if you come with me."

"Doc—"

But he didn't stop holding her or kissing her, so she ignored that advice until he was groaning and moving against her, too.

"*Inside.*"

This time she let him haul her to her feet and bring her into the darkened lab. He propped her up against the nearest wall and closed the back door, setting the alarms. As soon as he'd done that, she grabbed him again and started to kiss him. His thigh shoved between hers and she rubbed herself against the hardness until he started to curse.

She opened her eyes. "Gods I'm so sorry, I don't know what's wrong with me, I'm just—"

"Mating with me?" His smile was crooked. "We are in that time zone aren't we?"

"Then find the medical supplies, there must be something to put me out."

"Not advisable. I need you awake in case anyone else attacks us."

She held his gaze, her whole body trembling as he continued to lean into her, his breathing as erratic as her own.

"Then tie me up somewhere and shut the door."

"Negative. I need you in my sight."

"Then what?"

"This is working just fine."

His mouth came down over hers with a savagery she hadn't expected, but she opened to him, her body turning molten with need under his hands. She gasped as he picked her up and took her into the locker room that adjourned the bathroom and snapped on the lights. And then he had her against the wall and he was stripping her out of the important bits of her clothing, the ones that barred his way to her sex and she was helping him and doing the same to him.

As soon as she was freed, he picked her up and brought her crashing down over his big hard cock, holding her there with one hand wrapped around her hips as they both fought to breathe. Then he started to move fast and she started to come and then there was nothing except the slap of flesh on flesh and sensation that bridged their minds and bodies in a red-hot circle of intimacy.

MAC CAME inside her and wanted to roar as his hot seed pumped endlessly into her warm welcoming cunt. If he was going to die, this was one hell of a way to go.

What the hell was wrong with him?

That first sane thought for quite a while had him lifting her off him and settling her down on one of the benches.

"We'll keep this professional, right?"

"Yes, of course."

Mac studied her bent head. "I'll give you all the sex you need, no strings attached for the duration of your mating period or until help arrives."

"That's very...generous of you." She hesitated. "If you're sure?"

"Not a problem, doc." He hoped he sounded more professional than he felt.

"I'll start the shower."

He'd set traps around the perimeter to warn him if anyone approached and he was fairly confident they'd got the first wave of Etruscans. He had no way of knowing if there would be more. He turned the shower on, stripped off his clothes and returned to the locker room only to see Doctor Neeve's delectable arse in the air, as she struggled out of her tiny pink panties.

Like a heat seeking laser, he came up behind her kneeling figure and grabbed her by the hips shoving his cock deep and just pounded into her. She reached around to grab his upper arm bracing herself against his thrusts as she came and kept coming until he was finally able to climax himself. He collapsed over her back, one hand cupping her breast and struggled to breathe. What the hell was going on? He was in the middle of an extremely dangerous military situation and all he could think of was fucking the good doctor until he ran out of come.

"Captain McNeill?"

He picked her up and carried her toward the shower. "Call me Mac."

She rubbed her face against his cheek. "I'm so sorry about this."

"It's hardly your fault I can't keep my hands off you."

"But it is." She cupped his cheek. "I'm in heat, and you can't help it. I didn't realize you were a telepath. I didn't think you'd be affected by me."

He set her down carefully in the shower and picked up the soap. Whatever she was doing to him, it was having a miraculous effect on his dick, which was again stiff and ready for round three. He rubbed a soap slickened hand over himself and groaned and she went down on her knees and reached for him. For the first time in his life, he prayed that he'd neither be attacked nor rescued for a very long time.

His knees were wobbling by the time she finished her exquisite torturing of his cock and balls and he was more than ready to carry her back to bed and sleep the night away. He shut off the shower and fetched a warm towel to wrap her up in. He didn't even want to cover up an inch of her skin. He wanted it on display for him so that he could touch her and fuck her at will.

God he was fucking insane! Where had that come from? He'd never been this possessive, even with Leah. The thought of his wife was enough to help him lay Dr. Neeve down on her bed and step away.

"I need to go and check our security status and call Nimbus."

She nodded and rolled onto her side so that she could see him more clearly.

He hesitated. "Will you be all right?"

"Yes. Will you come back?"

He nodded. "Keep your weapon handy, just in case."

He wasn't sure he could keep away. Setting his jaw, he forced himself to leave and shut the door. The first task was to check the security cameras around the base and the second to make sure his superiors knew the situation. Even if the Etruscans had cut off normal methods of communication he had the means to make contact with anyone he pleased.

The security cameras were down, but back up power was available. After a quick override of the systems he reinforced the force field around the base using a new system the Etruscans would not be able to penetrate. Unless they were already inside the perimeter. With a few choice curses, Mac donned his snowsuit, picked up his weapon and patrolled the area around the small station buildings. It was one way of making sure his dick froze and stayed out of commission. He gathered the corpses in a neat pile for disposal by whoever eventually turned up to rescue them.

Back inside, he nuked some coffee and took it through with him to the control room. He focused on the blank screen

"Captain McNeill to Major Kaiden. Priority code 777."

"Kaiden. Go ahead."

Even using his advanced and enhanced telepathic powers, the reply was faint. Mac quickly summed up the situation and waited for Kaiden to reply.

"Roger that. Will check air space for any unidentified ships or shuttles and determine where your Etruscans came from. Anything else?"

Mac considered that. *"Yes sir. Dr. Neeve is in her mating cycle."*

"Damn."

"I'm reluctant to sedate her in case we need to get out of here fast."

There was a definite pause, as if his commanding officer was conferring with someone else.

"Mac? The Etruscan shuttle has been detected and detained from sending any more personnel down to the surface. There is a storm coming through which will delay the ground response. On the assumption that you are safe where you are, we'll monitor the area 24/7 and alert you to any possible issues."

"And Dr. Neeve, sir?"

"We'd appreciate it if you could be a good soldier and do your duty by her."

Mac blinked. *"You mean you want me to take care of her mating issues?"*

"You're in command, Captain McNeill. Do whatever is necessary, over and out."

Mac sat back, If he wasn't mistaken, he'd just been given official government approval to fuck Dr. Neeve's brains out.

NEEVE SAT up and wrapped the sheet around her. She knew McNeill had returned to the post, but there was still no sign of him. He'd promised to come back. She cupped her breast and pinched her nipple. Gods she *burned*...

The door opened and she instantly went for her weapon but it was him, Mac as he'd told her to call him. She lowered the gun and he shut the door, and holstered his own weapon.

"Is everything okay?"

He studied her for a long moment. "Yes. They've found the Etruscan shuttle and shut it down. We should be safe until the rescue crew gets here."

"Which will be when?"

"There's a storm coming through." He raised his arms over his head and peeled off his snowsuit giving her the perfect view of his abs and flat stomach. Then he stepped out of his pants and she could see the heavy thrust of his erect cock. "It's going to be a while."

"Then you could safely knock me out."

He walked toward her, his gaze on the sheet she had clutched to her breasts. "If it's all the same to you, I'd rather fuck you when you're conscious."

She let go of the sheet. With a groan, he placed his hands on the bed and leaned forward until his mouth closed around her nipple. She gasped and reached for his cock, wrapping her hand around it and squeezing hard. Wetness coated her fingers as he sucked her and moved his shaft to the same rhythm of his mouth through the tight circle of her fingers.

His hand came off the bed, trailed over her hip and delved between her legs, separating out the slick folds of her sex, thumbing her clit and sliding his fingers deep. She came for him and he added two more fingers stretching her, making her push up against his questing hand.

She tugged on his cock and he let her pull him onto the bed and obligingly lay on his back while she straddled him. His breath hissed out as she lowered herself and took him deep, rocking against him in little circles until he was fully seated within her.

Neeve held still and looked down into his dark blue eyes. Her mind bumped his, seeking entry, but he wasn't ready to admit her yet. Perhaps he couldn't. Wouldn't that be for the best?

"What's wrong?"

His voice was guttural with need, his hand already splayed over her hip ready to guide her into the rhythm he wanted.

"I'm not used to doing this without a telepathic connection. It feels strange."

"I don't know how to open such a link."

She rocked her hips, felt his big cock jerk inside her. "You did it without thinking the first time. Now you are guarding your mind."

He sighed and she felt the subtle easing of his mental barriers. "Will this work?"

"Oh..." Neeve surged through his formidable defenses and started moving on his cock at the same time. "Oh Gods, *yes.*"

As she drove him higher and higher, his mind opened to hers and she fed him her emotional and physical reactions until he worked out how to do the same. Then she forgot about teaching him anything and simply shared the experience until she was coming so hard she screamed.

He rolled her over onto her back and held her there while he pounded into her. Each mighty stroke like a pendulum shaking the narrow bedframe until he lost his smoothness and simply fucked her, his hips slamming into hers, his pelvic bone grinding against her clit until she was just thought and sensation and red heat. He growled when he came his whole body shaking as his come flooded her.

Eventually he drew her over him again and they lay quietly, both too exhausted to do anything but breathe and inhale the scent of their coupling.

MAC WAS JUST NODDING off when she touched his cheek.

"I thought Earth didn't have any telepaths."

"Officially, we don't."

"Then what are you?"

"A classified military experiment."

"Your mind is..." She hesitated. "Like nothing I've ever encountered before. It's almost like a machine."

"That's exactly what it is—what I am. A mechanically and genetically enhanced human being." He touched her hair. "And that, by the way is top secret military information not to be shared with anyone."

"Then why did you tell me?"

"In my opinion, you have a right to know who and what is in your bed." He opened his eyes wide as another thought struck him. "I'm one of the only males on Earth who has the necessary stamina and telepathic ability to get you through this mating period. What a fucking coincidence that I happened to be assigned to the base you work at."

"It's also weird that my mating urges only resurfaced when there was a telepath around. I just didn't know it." Neeve murmured.

"It's not something I'm supposed to shout about."

"Why not?"

"Because as far as the Earth is concerned enhanced soldiers are dangerous, unpredictable and should be exterminated."

"Being a telepath doesn't make you dangerous. I come from a planet full of them and we're one of the most peaceful civilizations around."

"I think telepathic power frightens them…the government, I mean. They created something they couldn't control. They've been trying to disown and destroy us ever since."

"That's horrible." She pulled out of his arms and came up on one elbow to stare down into his face. Her long red hair drifted against his skin. "I didn't know anything about this."

"I'm glad to hear it." He let out his breath. "I should've realized what was going on sooner."

"You can still sedate me. I don't mind. I--"

He put a finger against her lips. "Dr. Neeve, whatever headquarters say, we might still be in danger. I need you conscious and alert."

"Then I'll go and sleep in the other room."

He wrapped his hand around her forearm and held her still. "You'll stay here with me, and that's an order."

"I'm not military, Captain McNeill."

"In this situation you are. I want you where I can see you, preferably underneath me."

"And what if someone turns up while I'm 'underneath you'?"

"I'll sense them long before it gets to that, and so will you." He slid his other hand over the lush curve of her ass. "Right now you only have two choices, take a nap or fuck me blind."

3

"ThEY'RE HERE."

Mac turned to Neeve who was already up and dressed in her snow gear. Her arms were crossed over her chest and her glorious hair was tied back in a tight bun. He wanted to walk over to her yank the pins out and watch it fall down her back. Then he'd wrap it around his hand, hold her close and fuck her again…

"*Captain McNeill.*"

"What's wrong?"

"I got that last thought of yours." She licked her still swollen lips. "You're not helping."

Fifteen minutes ago, those lips had been round his cock while she sucked him off in the shower. She was still edgy; he could feel her need flowing over him, calling him… His over-used cock throbbed like a toothache as he instantly thickened. Strictly speaking, they still had over twelve earth hours before she was out of her mating period. He instinctively cupped his balls.

"Holy God, woman, no wonder you need two males to satisfy you."

She looked away, her color high. "I can only apologize, Captain, if you felt unequal to the task."

This time he did go over to her. He put his hand under her chin so that he could stare into her eyes.

"I think I did damn well, considering, don't you?"

"Of course, even though you were coerced into it." Her gaze dropped to his torso and the thrust of his cock, which was all too evident in the thin snowsuit he wore. "Will you please go stand over there? I can't be this near you, and not want to—"

An image flashed in his head of him crouched over her, his dick just about to penetrate her cunt.

"That's not helping me either." He glanced at the perimeter screens. "Damn it, they'll be here in less than five minutes. I can't satisfy you properly in that time frame."

She placed her hand flat on his chest. "There's something you need to know about our link."

"The telepathic one?"

"Yes, it's not just going to go away. We'll probably be able to link up forever."

"Good to know."

He put some distance between them. He had no choice. Greeting his superior with a hard-on was bad enough, especially since the whole of SpaceCon knew what he'd been doing. He didn't want to be found balls deep in her.

"But, Mac, you don't understand—"

He held up his hand as an internal communication came through. *"Perimeter codes accessed. We'll be with you in less than a minute."*

"Yes, sir."

He recognized that voice. Had Kaiden, the commander of the old unit, come in person? If so they really were trying to keep things quiet.

"Get your stuff, doc."

She stared at him for a long moment and then slowly nodded and turned toward the lab, her head held high.

"Neeve?"

"Yes?" She looked back over her shoulder at him.

"I'm glad we got you through this."

"We're not quite through it yet."

She smiled at him and it was all that he could do not to run over, scoop her up in his arms and take her back to bed.

The exterior door beeped a warning and suddenly the small space was full of soldiers and medics. Mac instinctively raised his weapon until he recognized a familiar towering figure in a dark blue uniform. Commander Kaiden Rostov was an intimidating sight. Two and a half meters tall and built like a linebacker, he instilled fear from a distance, an impression that remained when one got close enough to see his cold grey eyes and brutal mouth.

"Captain McNeill."

Mac saluted. "Sir."

"Where's Dr. Neeve?"

"In the lab, sir, retrieving her gear."

"Good." Kaiden nodded. "The security team will clean up here. I'll take you and the doctor back with me for debriefing."

"Yes, sir." His superior had already turned aside. Mac went still as Kaiden's gaze fixed on the doorway where Neeve was just emerging.

She had noticed the gigantic man too and stopped walking. If Mac had hackles, they would be rising as Kaiden's incredible mind reached out to Neeve.

"Doctor."

Neeve's gaze went to him, and then back to Kaiden.

"He's like you?"

"He's the original."

Kaiden frowned. *"Are you talking to her?"*

"Yes, sir, can't you hear us? I can hear both of you quite clearly."

"I can hear you individually, but only a faint buzz when you are communicating with each other. It's too fast. What the hell does that mean?"

"I have no idea, sir." Mac didn't care. He was just glad Kaiden was missing out. "Are you ready to leave Dr. Neeve?"

"Yes. I've lost some of the data, but the rest of it survived."

"As did you." Kaiden smiled down at her. A sight that was so unreal that Mac had to do a double take. "Which is the most important thing." Hell. Was his commander actually *flirting?*

"Only thanks to Captain McNeill. He saved my life."

"He's good at that. He saved my life once, too." He patted her shoulder. "Let me tell you about it."

He stepped aside to allow Neeve to leave the building, one hand on the small of her back. For the first time in his life, Mac contemplated shooting a superior officer. He found his pack and stood for a moment among the bustling soldiers. What the hell was wrong with him? He'd never felt this possessive of a woman before in his life. It went far beyond anything civilized and seemed to originate in some primitive part of his brain that just knew about fucking, breathing and surviving.

"Mac?"

Neeve was calling him and he wasn't about to leave her alone with Kaiden Rostov. He shouldered his pack and went out into the secured yard. Snow blasted into his face at an acute angle and the wind almost knocked him off his feet. The lights of a shuttle door were almost impossible to see even though the thing was barely 300 meters away.

He slogged over to the shuttle and got onboard, dumping his bag in the nearest safety harness to keep it secured during flight. It wasn't a large craft and could easily be piloted by the two of them. There were four small cabins, a communal eating and sitting area and some cargo space below.

Kaiden was already in the pilot's seat, running the pre-flight checks and communicating with the shuttle's computers and A. I. Mac studied the displays that were slowly powering up.

"Are you sure it's okay to leave?"

"No, but I want to put some distance between Dr, Neeve and this research outpost. If it becomes too dangerous, I'll set down and we can wait the storm out. It's only a fifteen minute ride back to Nimbus."

"Where is Dr. Neeve?"

"She'll be out in a moment." Kaiden glanced up at Mac. "Take the co-pilot seat. She can sit between us if she wishes, or crash in one of the cabins."

"Yes sir." Mac sat down and helped his commanding officer. He didn't need to turn his head to know when Neeve joined them. Beside him, Kaiden stirred, his nostrils flaring as if he was inhaling something he liked.

"Strap yourself in, Doctor." Kaiden said. "We're about to take off."

Mac returned his focus to the screens, relaying Kaiden's instructions to the A. I. as the craft struggled to get airborne in the high winds. Eventually they managed it and Mac settled down for the bumpy ride.

"It's no good." Fifteen minutes later Kaiden frowned at the monitors. "We can't get into the dock against this headwind. I've been around twice now." He glanced at Mac and then back at the doctor. "We'll have to put down at the emergency station at the end of the road to Nimbus and sit it out there."

"Yes, sir."

"Damn…" Neeve whispered.

"Is there something wrong, Doctor?"

Kaiden landed the craft with his usual skill and the retractable roof of the shelter immediately closed over them sealing them in from the worse of the elements. The shuttle whined as its engines cooled down and started to turn off.

"Does he know about me?"

Mac removed his headset. *"Yes."*

"And he's a telepath."

He turned around. *"So?"*

"We're in a very small space." She swallowed convulsively. Kaiden was looking from one of them to the other.

"You want him, too?" Mac stood up.

"I might."

"At least you're honest."

"It's not personal, you understand that. It's just a cultural and biological characteristic of my race."

"Sure." He knew he had no right to be insulted. Wasn't that the whole idea? He'd service her and she'd…fuck anything she could get her hands on.

She shoved her safety webbing to one side and shot to her feet. *"That's not true! I didn't know I was going to be trapped in a small place with two telepaths!"*

"What's going on, Captain?"

Deliberately blocking out Neeve, Mac answered his superior officer. *"Dr. Neeve is still in her mating cycle, sir."*

"Then go ahead and share a cabin. I'm sure I can find something to do while you complete your assignment."

"Thank you, sir."

Mac went over to Neeve who was still glaring at him. "Which cabin did you put your stuff in?"

"The first one, why?"

"Let's go."

He claimed her hand, gave his commander a quick nod and led her down the narrow hall into her cabin. Locking the door he started to strip, his cock rising to the occasion even though he was getting damned sore. She stripped out of her clothes so fast, he barely had a second before she was clinging to him and kissing him. Her nipples were hard points against his chest, her sex wet and warm as she rubbed herself over his thigh.

He managed to get them both on the bed and then he forgot

everything but being inside her again. He almost wanted Kaiden to see her like this, spread beneath him, urging him on as he fucked her. Even as he pistoned into her, he was aware of a sense of exhaustion creeping over him. He hadn't slept properly for three days. Perhaps she really did need two bodies to satisfy her. Was he man enough to accept that? What if he had a heart attack from the sheer fucking pleasure of it?

He came and for the first time in his life it hurt to climax, his come was sparse and hot, each spurt burning as it forced its way out of him. With a groan he rolled onto his back and closed his eyes. Perhaps he needed to get things into perspective. He was just doing his duty. She'd already made it clear that there was no future in the relationship, so why the hell was he trying to tell her who or what she could fuck?

"If I can't satisfy you right up until the end, go and ask Kaiden."

She cupped his face in her hands and waited until he opened his eyes. Hers were full of tears.

"Thank you."

She touched his cock and he yelped. "Actually, you should do it right now. For the first time in my life, I think I've run out of come."

She reluctantly released his shaft. "Why don't you sleep for a while and I'll return later?"

"I'll do that. But come back, all right?"

"Yes."

His eyelids felt like lead and he was half asleep before she'd even left the room.

NEEVE TOOK A REALLY LONG warm shower and wrapped herself in the military regulation bathrobe she found in a drawer in the bathroom. She managed to idle away another hour or so combing out her hair and drying it, but Mac was still sleeping. He looked exhausted and she didn't want to wake him. He'd already given her his all and there *was* another telepath on the shuttle with her.

She hesitated at the cabin door, her gaze drawn back to Mac. It was damned hard to leave him, harder than she'd anticipated. She felt, *connected* to him in a Pavlovan way, which made no sense and would have no meaning or context to him anyway. The thought of him agreeing to become part of a Pavlovan triad was so remote it was almost laughable.

And then there was that whole stupid 'destiny' thing she had with the Oracle of Pavlovan…

He'd done his duty by her, and that was probably more than enough for him to want to deal with. He'd only offered sex. But, *was* there more? Did she *want* more, or was it just because his particular brand of telepathy was so different to her own? Perhaps it would be better if she did seek out another human mate. At least then she'd know whether she would react to them both in the same way. Knotting the sash on her robe she finally managed to leave Mac to sleep and headed to the kitchen. She was hungry as well as horny, so maybe eating would substitute for her other hungers.

"Oh."

She flattened a hand against her chest as she turned the corner and almost fell over Commander Kaiden's big bare feet, which were propped up on the back of one of the kitchen chairs. His reaction time was so fast he was on his feet and holding her elbow before she'd barely had time to draw a breath. When she did breathe, she inhaled telepathic human male and felt dizzy. He was even taller than Mac and twice as wide. His almost white hair was cut brutally short as if its unusual color offended him.

"I'm sorry, Doctor Neeve. I wasn't expecting company." He retained hold of her elbow. "Is everything all right?"

"Captain McNeill's asleep."

She wondered if he'd make any crude jokes about that, but he said nothing. Easing out of his hold, she walked over to the food dispenser deliberately turning her back on him.

He cleared his throat. "But he's okay?"

"I assume so. He's hardly slept for the last three days."

She studied the menu and sighed. The shuttle might look newly fitted out, but the meals it was offering were still standard military fare and hardly appetizing. She selected the soup and waited until the cup was dispensed to her. Turning around she took a seat opposite Commander Kaiden at the table.

He'd taken off his outer uniform and snow gear and wore a tight grey T-shirt and a pair of sweats. Despite the informality of his dress, he was still formidable. As she blew and sipped at the soup he rocked back on his chair until it was on two legs and contemplated her.

"You weren't tired yourself?"

"I'm tired, but I can't sleep yet. I'm still too restless. My mating cycle doesn't end for another few hours."

"Didn't Mac tell you to wake him if you needed him?"

She finally gave up the pretense of just sitting there and raised her eyes to meet his. "No, he told me to come out here and find you."

"For what purpose?"

"You're a telepathic male and, in my present condition, I'm obviously susceptible to human telepaths."

"So you want to borrow my cock." His expression didn't change but he slid one hand down to his groin and cupped himself. "I'm way ahead of you."

Neeve blinked at him. "Mac said you would be."

He slowly brought the chair down to the floor. "Then come and take what you need."

Neeve pushed in her chair and came around the table to stare down at him. His eyes were a very pale grey like the finest unpolished silver. She stood between his legs and slowly took off her robe. His pupils widened as his gaze dropped to her breasts and her sex. Without speaking, he stripped off his T-shirt and lifted her astride him. She moaned as her mound met the rough cotton of his pants and rubbed herself against the hard ridge of his covered cock.

With a stifled sound, he dropped his head to her breast and took her nipple in his mouth, sucking her strongly in time to the motion of her circling hips. She arched into him, her body already sensitive from Mac's lovemaking, and rocked until she came hard, gasping out her pleasure. His pants were now damp and he struggled to pull them down far enough to reveal the blunt thrust of his big cock.

"Oh..." She sighed as she studied the thick head and bent to lick the pre-cum emerging from the slit. He groaned, his hips thrusting upward as if demanding she took more of him. She slid off his knees and knelt between his thighs and sucked as much of him in her mouth as she could, wrapping a hand around the thick base of his straining cock. Big, so big she wanted to devour him whole.

She sucked hard and he growled, the sound vibrating through his whole body. His hand fisted in her hair and stayed put, a rigid controlling presence she craved. His other hand went to her breasts and played there, drawing her nipples tight and sending shivers of pure lust straight to her sex.

"Christ..."

She caught his telepathic thought and zeroed in on it, opening her mind to him in return. Like Mac, his telepathic presence was unique and so different to a Pavlovan that she wanted to know more. He reached down and lifted her up into the air with ease, his mouth suckling her breasts, the crown of his cock notched against her clit, a hard insistent presence that made her come again and angle her hips upward trying to force him lower.

He laughed, a low guttural sound, and held her still, her clit throbbing against the heavy tip of his cock.

"Please."

"Not yet."

He kept her suspended over him, his muscles taut and put out his tongue again to lick her nipple. With a soft sound he set his teeth on her. She came so suddenly her whole body shook with it. He groaned and lowered her a scant inch over the wide head of his shaft.

"More."

He bit her nipple harder and her breath hissed out.

"When I'm ready."

She tried to rock down on him, but he was just too strong for her to move. All her motion did was stimulate her clit even more. She gave up, panting and looked into his eyes.

"Please?"

He dropped his gaze to where they were barely joined. Holding her up one-handed, he used his fingers to circle her clit and pinched. She came so hard she bucked against him with the pleasure. His cock jerked and he slid her down another couple of inches. Gods, how big was he? Could she even take all of him? It was like being penetrated with a fist.

He groaned. *"Fuck, yeah. I'd like to do that to you, get my whole fist in you so you could fuck it."* He drew a shuddering breath. *"Have Mac fucking your ass at the same time."*

She dragged her gaze up to his and simply stared at him. He raised an eyebrow. *"You do take two males at the same time, don't you?"*

She nodded as he eased himself even deeper. "You like the idea? Me in your cunt and Mac in your ass." He groaned. *"Some other lucky guy filling your mouth with his cock...so you're fucking full of it, full of male, and the full of come."*

His grip tightened, pushing her down into the swell of his

cock, widening her, making her accept even more of him until she was gasping and writhing against him.

"*Yeah, take it now. Take it all.*" His hips bucked in an urgent demand and he was finally sheathed entirely in her. "*Damn.*"

He held her still, his big cock throbbing inside her until she tentatively eased down on him and relaxed a little. Not that she could give very far, she was too crammed full of him to do that. Gods he was big. How would it feel when he started to move? She was almost afraid to find out.

"So, here's that cock you wanted."

She opened her eyes to focus on his face while he spoke aloud.

"Big," she breathed.

"Damn, I hope so. I'm big all over." He licked his lips as she tentatively tightened her inner muscles around him. "I want to roll you onto that floor and fuck you, but I'm going to be patient, and let you take what you need this time."

She tightened around him again and he groaned softly.

"You think there will be a next time?" She rocked her hips enjoying the sensation of him filling her and braced her hands on his broad shoulders. "Oh that's nice."

He dropped his hands and wrapped them around the sides of the chair giving her the ability to move freely on him, which she took willingly. She lifted and lowered herself over the thick column of his rigid shaft gasping at the pleasure, enjoying his helpless enjoyment as his desire seeped into her consciousness, tangling with her mind and then joining her completely.

A beautiful mind and a telepath of extraordinary clarity, which made Neeve feel like a goddess. And so big, she could ride his cock to fulfillment all night.

"*Yeah, don't worry about hurting my feelings,*" he breathed. "*That's what I am, doc, just a big hard cock for you to play with for as long as you need it.*"

Keeping one hand on his shoulder, she cupped her breast

and pinched her nipple hard. He responded instantly, his mouth lowering to her other breast and giving her an equal amount of pleasurable pain. She left him to satisfy her there, and moved her fingers lower to pluck and play with her clit driving her into another climax that made her clench hard on his cock and clutch frantically at his muscled shoulder, her nails digging deep.

She was also aware that Mac was awake and deliberately opened her link to him, letting him experience what she was doing with Kaiden. She wasn't surprised when he appeared in the doorway, naked and aroused, his gaze fixed on their inter-locked bodies.

"Fuck her ass, Mac."

Mac looked at her. *"Neeve?"*

"Yes, please, yes."

He found the lube they'd used earlier and slicked it over his cock and then coated his fingers, probing her ass until she was writhing down on Kaiden's shaft screwing herself deeper onto him with every twist of her hips. Kaiden's big hands came down to her hips and held her there, tilting her up and back for Mac's penetration.

She was so turned on she didn't even flinch at the blunt entry of his cock into her ass. Mac took over the motion and Kaiden stayed still as a rock as they worked her between them. She'd had two males before, but never two with such different telepathic patterns. It was like discovering a whole new world.

When she started to climax, she couldn't stop. Kaiden stirred underneath her trying to thrust his hips, constrained by both her weight and Mac's motions.

"Dammit, I've—gotta come, I—"

His guttural roar set Mac coming too, and Neeve screamed into Kaiden's mouth as he kissed her. Her thoughts went red and her mind fused with the two males sending them all into a never-ending circle of intense pleasure.

Eventually Mac slid down to the floor and stayed there.

"I'm done. I'm totally spent." He managed to raise his head to stare at Kaiden. "I can't fuck another thing. Can you help her out?"

Kaiden nodded and rose to his feet with Neeve still clinging to him like a vine. She didn't protest as he took her into his cabin and straight into the shower, which barely contained them both. Propping her up against the wall, he washed her thoroughly, his big hands moving over her so gently she wanted to purr like a *feerkit*.

When he'd finished, he picked her up again wrapped her in a towel and deposited her on his bed. She just lay there on her back allowing the towel to do all the work of drying her and waited for him to turn off the shower and come back. He left the lights in the bathroom on, which barely illuminated the bed but it was enough for her to appreciate the sight of his big muscled body in motion.

He emerged rubbing his now spiked hair with a towel and then threw the cloth on the floor and advanced on the bed. His cock was already erect again and thrust upward toward his flat stomach. He slid one knee between her thighs as he unwrapped her from the towel like a parcel and then spread her legs wide with his hand.

She lay still and let him look at her, his hands following his gaze, shaping and testing her mouth, her breasts and her hips until she was straining toward him. He slicked a hand over his wet cock.

"I want this in your mouth but it'll have to wait until I fuck you again."

"You can do both."

"Not at the same time." He smiled down at her. "I'm just prioritizing at the moment. I'm good at that." He rubbed his thumb over her swollen clit. "I've never met a female telepath before. I never knew it could be like this."

"Like what?"

He touched her forehead with his lips. "Mind to mind, sharing the fuck in a continuous emotional, telepathic and physical loop."

"That's one way of putting it."

"It's not like that for you?" His pale eyes focused on hers.

"Between telepaths it's always good, but when you meet your mate, it's even better."

His smile was crooked. "If that's true, God knows how you survive. This is intense enough for me."

"And I'm very grateful to you."

He reared up over her and shoved his cock home in one strong thrust making her whimper. "Tell me that again when I've made you scream yourself hoarse."

***

"Mac?"

Commander Kaiden's voice. Mac opened one eye. He was facedown in his bed and everything hurt.

"I'm about to take off. The weather's cleared and we'll be docking the shuttle at Nimbus in less than a minute."

"Do you need me?"

"No. But we will be disembarking in a few and you'll be required for debriefing by central command."

Mac groaned. "Yes, sir. Is Dr. Neeve all right?"

"She's doing fine."

He rolled over onto his back. His commanding officer looked fit and very pleased with himself. Mack remembered the sensation of them both being inside Neeve and his cock twitched. Covering himself with his hand he sat up.

"I'll take a quick shower and I'll be right there." He hesitated. "The debriefing, sir. Do we mention Dr. Neeve's mating needs?"

"We mention them, but we don't need to go into details." Kaiden nodded. "I'll go and get the preflight checks started."

Mac found his way into the shower again and hastily washed. It felt like only five minutes since he'd last been in there, washing off the combined scents of Neeve, Kaiden and himself. He still couldn't believe that they'd all…

Damn. He forced himself to step out of the shower. Whatever had happened it was irrelevant now. He'd done his duty as had Kaiden. Dr. Neeve had been satisfied and kept alive. His job was *done*. He'd do well to remember that.

4

Mac opened the fridge and stared at the contents before shutting the door again. They'd been back at Nimbus for almost three weeks, one of which had been taken up with fucking military protocol that had left him wanting to scream. As a super soldier his actions were always suspect. He was sick of being treated like an unstable animal. It made him want to behave like one, which would, as Kaiden had calmly pointed out just prove the military's point that he should be eliminated.

At two in the morning, nothing looked very appetizing and the shit the military served up was a disgrace anyway. He checked how much coffee was left in the pot and how warm it was and decided to make a fresh pot. He'd need it if he were going to survive the next few days.

Kaiden had taken the majority of his men and gone back to London leaving Mac in charge of a base with new superior security and an increased compliment of highly trained guards. The majority of the scientists hated it. He couldn't even tell them why things had changed because he'd been ordered not to.

The consensus was that the Etruscans might try to take Dr. Neeve out again but no one was telling *him* why, even though he

45

was supposed to be in charge of her security detail. When he'd pressed Kaiden for information, his commander had stated he didn't know anything more than Mac, which was probably a lie as well, seeing as he'd gotten so cozy so quickly with the doc.

He sat down at the table and stared at the coffee maker. If it didn't hurry up and make the damned stuff he was going to start mainlining the powder up his nose.

Dr. Neeve was due another three days off for mating purposes soon. He'd dutifully reported the fact to Kaiden at HQ and been told they had the matter in hand and would be sending a Pavlovan volunteer to service the female.

Fuck that.

Mac snorted and went to get a mug for his coffee. Half the reason he couldn't sleep was because of waking up hard for her, wanting her, dreaming about her only to find the walls he'd deliberately erected against her in his mind held all too well. Either that or she was blocking him too, and he was a damn fine liar.

"Oh."

He looked over his shoulder wondering if he'd imagined her so clearly that he'd somehow summoned her presence.

"Doc." He cleared his throat. "I'm just making some coffee."

She nodded but lingered in the doorway.

His hand tightened on his mug. "Don't worry I'll go in a minute."

"You look tired."

He looked at her properly for the first time in weeks. She was wearing a blue robe over a pair of fleeceteck pajamas and pink socks.

"I'm the commander of this base and we're on high alert."

He tensed as she came further into the room and sat down at the table.

"And this increase in security is my fault." She pushed her long auburn hair out of her eyes. "I feel like such a burden.

There aren't any ships scheduled to return to Pavlovan for another few weeks, so I'm not even able to leave."

The thought of her going hit him somewhere low in the gut like the punch of a gunshot.

He slammed the coffee pot on the counter and the glass trembled. "I bet you can't wait to get home."

"Not really."

Ignoring his impulse to ask why, he held up the pot. "Do you want some?"

"Yes, please."

He poured her a cup and brought it over to the table. Fuck it, he was sitting down. He'd been there first. If she didn't like it she could always leave. He concentrated on adding sweetener to his coffee and stirring it in. Just sitting this close to her made him hard, made him want to inhale her warm scent instead of oxygen.

"I had a communication from Commander Kaiden about your next mating period."

"What did he say?"

"That he has the resources necessary to fulfill your requirements."

"Great." She put her cup down on the table very precisely.

"Then I suppose we'll be seeing him soon."

"I doubt that's what he meant."

"Oh yeah, I forgot. Humans aren't a reusable resource to you, are they? You probably need fresh meat." He gulped down the rest of his coffee, scalding his mouth and rose to his feet. "Excuse me."

She looked up at him. "What the hell is that supposed to mean?"

"Just a general comment about the difference between your race and mine."

"Oh, that's *right*. Humans are so *good* at staying with one person their whole lives, aren't they? How dare you criticize my behavior!"

"I can't speak for the entire human race, but I know that I was damn faithful to my partner. I have to assume that even if Malke had been around last month, you still would've fucked someone else as well."

"Then you would've been wrong. I never needed any other male when I had him."

Mac stopped walking. Did he deserve that low blow to his male ego? He should let it go.

"Sorry I wasn't man enough for you, princess."

She glared at him. "Do not *ever* call me that."

"Next time start with Commander Kaiden. He's obviously the right male for you."

He reached the door and just remembered to slam his coffee cup down on the counter. With one last glance at the doctor's rigid back he sauntered out into the hallway and stopped moving. He slowly let out his breath and stared unseeingly at the grey floor tile and then up at the ghostly strip lighting over his head.

Through his own anger, something reached him, a thread of feeling, of *pain* that made him turn around and go back into the kitchen. Closing the door behind him he leaned against it.

"Doc. I—should apologize. That was completely out of order."

She didn't move or speak. He walked around until he was in front of her. She had her face buried in her hands and her shoulders were hunched forward.

"Dr. Neeve?"

"I've never thought you were disposable."

"As I said, I apologize for my thoughtless comments about a society I know fuck all about."

"If you are Pavlovan, you are taught how to manage a Pavlovan mating cycle if the third member of your triad isn't available." She bit off the words as if she resented having to utter every single one of them.

"That makes sense."

"Sometimes we do need to use an unconnected third, but it is highly unusual for any Pavlovan to enter adulthood without being aware of at least one of his or her mates." She placed her hands palm down on the table and contemplated them. "Losing a mate is never easy. If I were on my home planet, I would be sent before the Oracle to be given another. I don't have that option here. I didn't even know there *were* any telepaths here. I thought I was all on my own."

He nodded even though she wasn't looking at him.

"To suggest that my pain in losing Malke was in any way less than yours in losing your mate was grossly unfair."

"I know."

She slowly raised her gaze to meet his. "Then why say it?"

He shrugged. "Because I was angry."

"I got that. What I don't understand is *why?*"

"Because I—" He closed his mouth and simply stared at her. There was no way in hell that he was going to admit he missed anything about her. What was the point? She was a security risk of gigantic proportions and it was his job to keep her safe until they got her off planet. And, despite telling him they'd been linked telepathically forever, she'd cut herself off from him so completely that he felt like there was a hole in his skull. It had taken all his psychic energy to do the same to her.

She put her coffee mug in the sink. She was so close to him that he could've reached out and yanked her hard against his chest and the swell of his cock. And then what? She didn't need him. It wasn't her mating cycle, so he was pretty damn useless.

She wrapped her arms around herself and straightened her spine.

"Will you let me out of here?"

He belatedly realized that he'd gone back to guarding the door and stepped to one side. "I apologize again."

She stalked past him, her chin in the air and walked off down the hallway toward her quarters. Mac stared after her and then returned to his seat and the table and buried his head in his hands.

That had gone well.

All he'd done was upset her because he was a fucking judgmental ass incapable of moving on from what had happened. She hadn't asked him to get all emotional around her, and she'd probably be mortified if she ever guessed that he had. Telling Neeve he'd never been unfaithful to Leah was the truth. He hadn't the nerve to tell Neeve the rest—that after fucking her; he didn't think he'd want anyone else again, either.

He was a fucking idiot. Which was highly appropriate.

With that in mind, he made his way back to his office and called up Commander Kaiden's message service. To his surprise, Kaiden picked up.

"Mac, is everything okay?"

"Yes sir." Mac rubbed a hand over his unshaven chin. "I have a question."

"Go ahead."

"Are you planning on coming up here for Dr. Neeve's mating cycle?"

"I don't think I have a choice. I was just about to contact you. The Pavlovan government has put a hold on any of its citizens traveling on Earth until the Etruscan issue dies down."

"Great."

"What's the problem?"

"If you're here, then I don't need to be. I'm requesting five days leave." He made it a statement rather than a question.

"Mac—"

"She'll be fine with you."

"Request denied. You were her first contact. I require you to be there in case you're needed."

Mac set his jaw. "And if Dr. Neeve doesn't want me there?"

There was a definite pause. "Has she said that?"

"If she doesn't require my presence, I'll ask her to contact you. Over and out." Mac shot to his feet and shoved back his chair. He might as well ruin the rest of the night and go and get that confirmed by Dr. Neeve. Somehow he doubted it would be a problem for her to give him his marching orders.

***

NEEVE SAT on the side of her bed and scowled before jumping to her feet and pacing the small space again. What was it about Captain McNeill that made her behave like a bitch? She wanted to slap his face, scratch his skin until it bled, and then climb on top of him and ride his cock until he begged for mercy.

She wanted him to be like a Pavlovan mate. Wanted all of him, mind, body and will. And he thought she saw him as some kind of disposable sperm dispenser. She went back over their conversation in the kitchen. Where had it all gone wrong? Why couldn't she have reached out to him telepathically or even physically?

Because she was a coward. Losing Malke had been bad enough. She'd felt like someone had ripped out her heart. Messing around with a human telepath with extraordinary powers was just stupid when there was no future in it. They'd made a deal to keep their relationship sexual. That was it. If she wanted more, she was just asking to be hurt all over again. She had to protect herself.

A knock on her door has her spinning around. "Who is it?"

"Captain McNeill."

She let out her breath and retied the sash of her robe. "Come in."

He entered, his gaze dropping to the security panel beside the door. "Don't tell me you left it unlocked."

She tapped her skull. "I just opened it. I can manipulate power circuits from here. What do you want, sir?"

"Commander Kaiden just informed me that he can't get a Pavlovan up here to mate with you, but he will be coming himself." His mouth curved up at the corner. "No pun intended."

"Why can't he get a Pavlovan?"

"Your government is on high alert and won't let anyone travel."

She turned away from him and pretended to adjust the blind. "Okay, thanks for telling me. I estimate I'll go into my mating cycle in about five days."

"I'll let him know."

She waited, but he didn't leave.

"There's one more thing. If Commander Kaiden is here, you won't need me, will you?"

She closed her eyes and wrapped her arms around herself.

"If that's the case, and I assume it is, will you contact him in the morning and tell him so? He'll want to hear it from you rather than me."

Slowly she swung around to face him. "You told him that you didn't want me?"

"No, I told him that *you* didn't want *me*."

"And how did you work that out? Was it before or after we fucked each other so hard that you ran out of come?"

He went still like the predator he was and his eyes narrowed but not before she'd caught the gleam of lust.

"Wasn't I good enough for you, Captain McNeill? Damn I feel so *disposable*." She set her teeth and glared at him so hard it hurt. She marched over to him and stuck her finger in his face. "You'd bloody better be here when I'm mating because this time I'm going to suck you dry until you're nothing but a broken husk. *Then* you can crawl away and die."

The next second was a blur as he reached for her and slammed her against his hard body. His mouth descended and she opened hers to him, biting and nipping at his lips as he tried to kiss her.

"Goddamit, keep still!"

She bit even harder and he cursed, his hand tangling in her hair and cupping her skull until she was exactly where he wanted her. He pinned her against the door and she was aware of every muscular inch of him from knee to shoulder. The kiss went on and on, turning into something so needy and filthy and spectacular that her knees started to give way. He grabbed her hand, placed it over the front of his pants and she gripped him hard through the fabric.

"I thought you said you didn't want me, Mac?"

He pushed into her hand and she squeezed hard until he yelped.

"You closed your mind to me."

"Because you made it quite clear that you'd done your duty and that was an end to it."

"And it was. It is. It has to be."

"Then what's this, then, Mac?"

"Residual lust?"

She moaned as he slid his hand inside her pajama bottoms and curved his strong palm around her ass cheek.

"It's not that simple."

"It never is for a woman." He braced one hand on the wall beside her head so that she couldn't look away from him. "I'm supposed to be guarding you until you leave Earth. That's my primary mission. I was chosen because I'm a telepath and a super soldier."

"And I'm leaving in a few weeks."

"Yes," he stared into her eyes. "We both know where we stand. There's no future in this for either of us."

She nodded, but neither of them made any effort to let each other go.

"And yet, I still want you." Mac murmured.

"I got that." She licked her lips and then his. "And I want you, even though you might remember that I'm not in my mating cycle."

He groaned and buried his face in the crook of her neck. It was a good thing that he was still holding her up because her body turned liquid.

"Don't say that. You're supposed to slap my face and tell me to fuck off."

"I'll tell you to fuck me, if you like."

His hand scooted lower over her ass and slid down to her sex. "Christ you're wet."

She arched her back and his fingers pushed higher over the throb of her clit and lingered there, slowly rubbing back and forth as she rocked against him. With a low sound he penetrated her with his thumb and held still.

"Please fuck me, Mac."

It was stupid and they both knew it, but she couldn't stop the words.

"Damn..."

He picked her up and sat her on the side of her bed. She gripped the frame as he stripped with fast, economic movements that left her staring at his tight abs and rigid cock. With a sigh, she leaned forward and tasted him with her tongue, licking at the wetness gathering at the tip of his crown.

He slid one hand into her hair and surged forward, urging her to take more of him, but she continued just to play, licking and kissing him like an ice cream until he was even wetter. She pointed her tongue and wiggled it into his slit and he made the most wonderful sound, a mixture of need and frustration that sank into her like the finest Pavlovan spirits.

"Suck me."

She ignored his urgent command and continued to torment him with her tongue. With a growl he flipped her onto her back and higher onto the bed. He buried his face between her legs, nuzzling her soaking folds with his mouth and the scrub of his stubbled chin.

Shifting his weight, he guided his shaft toward her mouth, groaning as this time she took him in and set her lips around his thick length drawing him deeper with every pull. His mouth plundered her sex, his fingers joining the delights of his probing tongue until she was coming all over his face, grinding herself against the hard lines of his jaw as he started to fuck her mouth.

"Not yet."

She didn't understand his words until he pulled away from her and flipped her over onto her stomach. Instinctively she came up on her knees. He pulled her back to the edge of the bed, stood on the floor and grabbed her hips.

"Now I'll fuck you."

His cock slid home in her cunt and he started to thrust hard. One hand braced over her shoulder holding her in position as he fucked her. The other roamed her breasts and hips and finally settled over her clit rubbing and circling her now tender nub until she screamed into the pillow and came so hard she felt the echo of the shock scream back from his mind.

He kept on fucking her and she started to fight him, aware that he was driving her toward a place that she'd never found with Malke and desperately feared. She almost forgot how to do anything but breathe, her mind as open to him as her sex, his thoughts as clear as her own, both of them fused together in the pursuit of immense sexual pleasure.

This shouldn't be happening, this *couldn't* be happening, not with him, not with—.

"God, Neeve."

She reached back to grab his wrist and dug her nails in as he continued to pound into her. She couldn't stop coming now, and he couldn't stop feeding the emotions back to her and—

"Fuck." He rammed himself deep and held there as the hot pulses of his come filled her.

She'd lost her mind to him completely and could no longer tell where he stopped and where she began. For a moment he held himself rigidly over her his chest heaving as if he'd run a race.

While he recovered she made a faint attempt to gather the frayed corners of her mind and stitch them back together again. But it was impossible. He seemed to have entered her consciousness at a molecular level and would not leave...

She let him rearrange them both on the bed. Him on his back, and her on her side curled against him. Her hand rested on his chest and her right knee cradled his muscular thigh.

"Mac."

"Mmm..."

"We can't keep doing this."

"Dammit, woman I was enjoying the moment." He groaned. "Can we just wait a few minutes before we have *that* discussion?"

She kept talking. "Every time we have sex, our telepathic link gets stronger."

"I'm not the best person to judge that statement. My thought processes are entirely controlled by my dick at the moment."

"It's wrong, Mac. I'm not *supposed* to feel anything for you except sexual relief."

"You're not in your mating phase, so maybe this is different."

His tone was more serious now as if he too was considering what was happening more carefully.

"I shouldn't be attracted to you at all when I'm not in my mating cycle. You're not even a *Pavlovan*."

"But I'm a telepath." He sighed. "I can't imagine not making love to a telepath now." He flinched. "Ouch."

Her fingernails dug into his flesh. She didn't want him thinking about any other female but her, let alone a telepathic one.

"Which is why we have to stop," Neeve said firmly.

He came up over her and stared down into her face. She wanted to lick a path down his skin all the way to his cock and start again...

"I'm not sure if I can do that."

She studied the set of his jaw and the resolution in his dark blue eyes. "Do you *want* to be in a Pavlovan triad?"

"What do you mean?"

"Would you be willing to share me with another male, or another female on a permanent three-way basis?"

"Three-way?" He made a face. "Are you suggesting we'd all be fucking each other even those of the same sex?"

"That's exactly what I'm saying." She held his gaze. "All three members of the mating triad decide who gets to have sex with whom, and they don't get jealous about sharing."

His expression hardened. "I don't share."

"Which is why I'm telling you that we can't keep doing this. I can't imagine committing to just one person."

"Fuck." He rolled onto his back and stared up at the ceiling. "You're right." He sat up and managed to get off the bed. "This *will* have to stop." He stooped to pick up his clothes giving Neeve a perfect view of his perfect ass. "Call Kaiden tomorrow and tell him you need someone else and that you don't want me."

She bit down hard on his lip as he methodically put on his clothing. She daren't reach out for his mind, which she suspected was as battered and defenseless as her own.

He turned back at the door, his expression grim. "I'm sorry."

"For what?" Better to use words than thoughts, better to protect themselves.

"For not being the man that you want."

"I want you."

"And I can't exist in a threesome."

"I understand. It's outside your culture's idea of the norm." She gathered the sheets around her and nodded, giving him permission to walk away. "Good night, Captain McNeill."

He briefly closed his eyes and then left leaving her staring at the closed door. What happened if you met your mate who wasn't even Pavlovan, and they turned you down? She had no idea. It never happened. Maybe her mother would know what to do, but the last person she wanted to confide in at the moment was her mother. She'd never countenance Neeve's infatuation with a human...

She curled up into a ball and closed her eyes. After Malke died she'd thought she'd never smile again, let alone have sex, and now she'd done both. Dammit, why did emotional stuff have to be so hard? Believing Malke could love her for herself and not for her family connections had been difficult enough. But he'd proved it by being willing to walk away from Pavlovan and follow her to Earth. She'd always wanted to be free of her family and against all the odds she'd managed it. It was ironic that she'd now met a male who had no idea who or what she was and probably wouldn't care even if he did know. She swallowed hard. Perhaps she'd been right all along and that was all she was, a prize to be won and without that lure she wasn't good enough for anyone...

She'd survive this, go back to Pavlovan visit the Oracle and find a new mate. If she could get Mac out of her system...

That was the part she was finding difficult.

5

MAC FINISHED PACKING AND WENT OUT TO MEET THE INCOMING
shuttle. He'd managed to occupy himself with work for the past
few days and hadn't seen Neeve at all. She'd done as he'd asked
and contacted Kaiden for him to be removed from her pool of
mating material. Forcing himself to rebuild his psychic shields
had been much harder than not seeing her. He yearned for her
like some stupid teenage crush and wanted to be with her all the
time.

"Dammit." Mac muttered. "This is the best way."

"I beg your pardon?"

Kaiden stood at the doorway of the shuttle, his large frame
filling the space. The snow was falling heavily and a thick white
mist had descended over the base making it difficult to tell the
ground from the air.

"Sir." Mac snapped out a salute.

"Captain McNeill." Kaiden's gaze fell to Mac's backpack. "I
need to speak to you before you leave." He stepped out of the
way. "I've also brought someone you know."

Mac went still as one of his least favorite people on the
planet stepped out from behind Kaiden's vast bulk.

"Captain McNeill."

"Professor Dean."

"It's good to see you again, Captain." The professor's dark eyes scanned Mac's face. "I need to run some tests before you can leave."

"I'm no longer in your program. It was dissolved."

Professor Dean looked back at Kaiden who had remained by the now closed door.

"The professor has authority to examine you, McNeill."

"Who from?"

"The Commander in Chief."

Kaiden's shields were so high that Mac could get nothing out of him. He saw the disdainful glance Kaiden gave the professor and knew that he wasn't the only one who trusted the scientist about as much as a used plutonium salesman. Which was odd, because Kaiden had always been the great believer in the program--the one who'd insisted everything would turn out right.

Mac let out his breath. "The medical lab is through here, Professor."

He led the way through to the medical wing only to find that the professor's entourage were already milling around the space and making it their own. He didn't recall giving anyone permission to install new tech into the lab, but he suspected his protest would be ignored.

Professor Dean's arrival meant the minions scattered, leaving Mac alone with the woman. She settled at one of the terminals and glanced at him.

"Strip please."

Mac took a deep breath. "Why is that necessary?"

"I need to do a whole body scan."

"For what purpose? I'm officially on leave."

"As you've already been notified, your leave has been

cancelled by the authority of the Commander in Chief. Do you want to be court-marshaled?"

Mac held the professor's gaze. "To be honest? At this point, I don't really give a shit about continuing my military career as long as you keep your hands off me."

"If you are court-marshaled and found guilty, you won't be allowed to go free and live a normal life. Who would want a super soldier living next door? You'll be sent to my lab, and I'll *own* you."

"I'd rather commit suicide."

"And if you attempt that, you'll be considered mentally unstable and I'll be empowered to round up all the other males who were in the program with you and have them exterminated as a threat to our great nation." She paused. "Is that what you want?"

He simply stared at her, his hands fisting at his sides.

She smiled. "But it doesn't have to come to that, does it, Captain McNeill? Just stay here, mate with Dr. Neeve for three days for the next two months and allow me to monitor any changes in your abilities after each event."

"You don't get to monitor us during the 'event'. Only me, afterward."

She nodded. "Agreed. Now strip and lie down on the gurney."

"Dr. Neeve?"

Neeve looked up from her work and found Commander Kaiden looming in the doorway.

"Commander."

He stepped inside her office and shut the door. "May I have a word with you?"

"Sure." She tried to smile. "Is it about my mating cycle? Has Captain McNeill left?"

"He's still here." He met her gaze. *"There's been a problem. The military authorities have decided he must remain as your primary contact during your remaining two mating cycles."*

"He decided not to go?" She fiddled with her microscope. *"What's going on? He doesn't want to be with me. It's not a good situation for either of us."*

Kaiden took his time sauntering over to her desk and pulling out a chair. *"I suspect he had no choice. The scientific director of the super soldier program is here and she is determined to add new data to her existing profile of Mac."*

"I think I talked him out of it." Kaiden smiled. "I'll be here, too, as back up."

"That's good to know. *Can't he get out of it?"*

"He says not."

"Damn, this is bad." She forced herself to pat Kaiden on the arm. "I really appreciate your willingness to help me out here. *Can you go first? Can we lessen the impact on Mac?"*

"You're more than welcome, Dr. Neeve." Kaiden stood up and held out his hand. *"Just let me know when you need me. And I'll try and make sure Mac is the one kept as back up."*

Commander Kaiden brought her hand to his mouth and kissed it lingeringly, but she knew it was just an act. He wasn't as attached to her as Mac had been after one mating session, and she wasn't feeling more than pleasurable sexual anticipation about him. For whatever reason, Mac was different and she had to protect him.

"Mac."

He woke up from a troubled sleep to find Kaiden at his door.

"Neeve's ready for us."

He rolled out of bed and rubbed his eyes. Whatever stuff Professor Dean had forced into him was still making him feel like crap.

"What's wrong?" Kaiden had his shields so high that the question barely squeaked through.

"I'm not sure." Mac attempted to run a diagnostic on his own systems. *"She's messed with something. I feel all...wrong."*

"The prof? I'll see if I can pick up anything."

"Yeah, do that."

"Then we'd better keep this convo to the minimum. Tell Neeve."

Mac nodded. Kaiden was the only person who'd noticed that his telepathic link with Neeve was more complex than his link with anyone else. He only hoped to God that Kaiden hadn't told Professor Dean or that the witch hadn't worked it out for herself. She'd always taken special pleasure in making Mac's life hell probably because he'd been the first one to question her methods-the first one to realize the enormity of what she'd done to them and fight to get free.

"Come on."

Kaiden walked ahead of Mac down the white hallway and turned toward the guest suites. "They've put us in here. I guess the beds are bigger."

"Great."

Kaiden entered a code and they both went through the door into the executive suite, which was usually reserved for visiting dignitaries. It was fitted out in sleek modern furniture in shades of white and beige. Neeve was sitting in one of the chairs, her arms wrapped around herself and her head lowered. She looked up as the men entered, but she didn't smile.

"Dr. Neeve." Mac nodded at her and took the seat furthest away. "How are you?"

"Would either of you like a drink?" Kaiden asked as he headed into the small kitchen that adjoined the living area. "I'm parched." He made a lot of noise rattling around in the refrigerator and banging cupboard doors looking for glasses.

Neeve glanced at Mac. *"There's something wrong."*

"What?"

She frowned. *"With this space. I feel like I'm being watched."*

"I just had a similar conversation with Kaiden about what's going on in my head."

She studied him for a second. *"There's definitely something going on. I'll block harder."*

"Hell, you can control electrical fields, can't you?" Mac smiled. *"Can you take security systems out?"*

"Yes."

"Then when we get naked, you go ahead and do that. It might not stop the prof for long, but it will give us a chance for some privacy."

She raised her chin. "Kaiden's going first this time, okay?"

His smile faded. "Are you sure that's what you want?"

"I thought you'd prefer it. You were the one who asked to be off base while this happened."

"You know why I did that." He turned his gaze to Kaiden who was still messing around in the kitchen. "Is there any beer?"

"I'll check,"

"Thanks." Mac stretched out his legs and sighed. "If I'm going to be hanging around I might as well get comfortable.

Neeve's gaze drifted down over his body and his cock jumped to attention. "There's another reason why you're better off being last."

"And what's that?" Mac rubbed a casual hand over his chest and then down to cup his balls. Why he felt the need to display himself to a female he'd sworn to keep away from he couldn't say.

"Pavlovan sex works better as a threesome and I already know how you feel about those."

She was talking more loudly than usual. Was she attempting to convey something to Professor Dean who he was sure, despite her promises, was hanging on their every word?

"What are you trying to say, Doc?"

Neeve shrugged. "You told me you don't like to share."

"I think you're forgetting that Kaiden and I already *have* shared you, Dr. Neeve."

"Not entirely. And once was apparently enough to freak you out. What did Commander Kaiden do? Touch your ass or something?"

He shrugged. "Maybe I don't have the hots for him."

"So why can't you come to bed with us, and just share me? I'm not asking you to fuck him."

Mac shuddered. "Fuck *that*? No thanks."

"Hey." Kaiden called out in his deep voice. "I'm fucking irresistible. Ask anyone."

Neeve rose to her feet and came toward Mac. "Fine, then wait it out. *That should give your scientists something to think about.*"

His gaze fastened on the v of her blue robe and the intriguing shadow between her breasts. He licked his lips and silently groaned. The thought of her having Kaiden and not him first was difficult to swallow. She belonged with him. Didn't she see that?

"I see it, Mac. You're the one who won't believe it."

She walked over to Kaiden in the kitchen and let her robe fall to the ground. She was naked beneath the silk. With a grin, Kaiden picked her up and sat her on the countertop, spreading her legs with his hips and sliding one hand into her hair as he kissed her.

Mac tried to look away as a low growl rumbled from his throat. Kaiden's big hand cupped Neeve's ass and drew her closer and closer to the roll of his hips. Even from his seat, Mack could smell the scent of their arousal all around him.

"Mmm..." Kaiden murmured. "I have too many clothes on."

He wrapped an arm low around Neeve's hips and lifted her off the countertop. "Mac, get your own beer. I have to service Dr. Neeve right now." He walked out of the kitchen and down the hallway to the bedroom, Neeve clinging to him like a vine.

Mac didn't hear the door close and that was bad enough, but then Neeve started to gasp and moan and he seriously wanted to go in there and fucking shoot his commanding officer through the head, He knew he was doing the right thing— keeping away from her, letting Kaiden take the brunt of the mating cycle and he didn't fucking care. *He* wanted to be the one inside her, making her moan, making her come.

He shot up from the couch and then slowly let out his breath as the noises of frantic sex continued. She had three days to get through. He'd have his turn, and if he waited, he'd prove to Professor Dean that his presence at the station hadn't been necessary at all.

In the kitchen, he opened the fridge and found a few bottles of beer stacked in the door side. It wasn't a brand he liked, but it might help him drown his sorrows for a few hours as Kaiden and Neeve... Damn. He opened one beer and drank it down in one.

"So how long do you think he'll last?" Kaiden asked.

Neeve looked down at him. She was currently full of his cock and enjoying straddling his torso as she slowly rode him in lazy circles of her hips.

"Mac?"

"Who else?" He winced as she deliberately tightened her internal muscles around his fast recovering shaft. "Damn, you are one demanding female."

"Don't start complaining." She smoothed a hand over his muscular chest, pausing to circle his nipple. "I was just going to comment about how popular you'd be on Pavlovan with your current unattached status."

His smile was complacent. "I'm good aren't I?"

"You've got a nice big cock and you can last for hours, which makes you perfect for Pavlovan sex."

"I wish I could go there." His smile disappeared. "Since I've had sex with you I can't imagine ever being satisfied with a partner who isn't telepathic."

"You do understand that we have sex with everyone?"

"Yes. Mac told me."

"Does it offend you—the thought of maybe being with another man?"

"No. I've realized that it isn't just about the physical, but the mental as well." He smiled. "Of course I'm pretty damn sure I'd naturally attract two beautiful female telepaths, just like you."

"Flatterer."

"I mean it." He cupped her jaw. "You are extraordinary in so many ways."

"Damn, I wish I'd bonded with you."

"That would be far too easy." His hips rolled against hers and she realized he was fully erect again.

Neeve studied his handsome face. "I could ask if you like."

"Ask what?"

"If I could bring you home with me."

"You could do that?"

"I'm...connected to some fairly important people there."

"But we're not mated."

"So what? I think I'm mated with Mac, but he doesn't seem to agree."

Despite the throb of his cock inside her, he concentrated on her face. "Would you take Mac, too?"

"I'd love to." She sighed. "But I don't think he quite sees it like that."

"Have you asked him?"

"Kaiden, he's sitting out there drinking himself into a stupor rather than have sex with me."

"He thinks he's doing the right thing and with Professor Dean being here he might have a point."

"Who is she exactly?"

"She's the head of our disbanded program. She recruited us all into the team, but she's always had a thing about Mac and used him as her primary scientific guinea pig. I'm not surprised he hates her guts."

"How many of you are there?"

"A few." He shrugged. "Less than ten still alive."

"It must be lonely for you here."

He wrapped a hand around her waist and impaled her firmly on his cock. "Yeah, now can you concentrate on something else for five minutes?"

"Of course. If five minutes is all you can last."

With a smile she bucked against his restraining grip and then gasped as he flipped her onto her back and started fucking her. She wrapped her legs over his tight ass and held on. Her whole being focused on what he was doing with his cock and the first delicious sparks of her upcoming orgasm. He was much heavier and bigger than her and held her pinned to the bed with his large frame and the relentless pounding of his hips against hers.

She smiled against his shoulder and then bit him hard as he gripped her ass in his hands and brought her more firmly against him, coming up on his knees and shortening his stroke until each thrust sent a burst of sensation against her clit.

"God...I love fucking you."

"Mmm..."

She started to climax around him and simply let it happen without forcing anything, reveling in the clench and release of her cunt as she milked him until his come spurted deep inside her. She let her mind open to him and showed him how good she felt, experienced the burst of his own raw pleasure in all its masculine intensity.

Sometimes not being mated to a male made the sexual experience more bearable and less complicated. As Neeve came down from her high, she wondered whether that was better—not to feel so intensely—to just enjoy the physical relationship and the telepathic sharing a man like Kaiden could provide. Would that satisfy her long term? It would certainly protect her heart… If Mac remained on Earth, sex without commitment might have to do.

KAIDEN LAY ON HIS BACK, his arms and legs spread wide as if in surrender. Neeve bit his nipple and he groaned. "Give me a few more minutes."

She bit him again just to watch his whole body shudder.

"You're slowing down, Commander."

He opened one pale blue eye and regarded her. "I'm a super soldier, not a god."

"I noticed that." She pretended to sigh. "I'm going to see what Mac's up to."

"Good luck."

She found her robe and put it on. "I'll probably need it."

"Bring him back for round two."

"If I can."

He opened both eyes, his expression serious. "Doc, he needs you. I'm willing to do whatever it takes to make him comfortable with me sharing the same bed."

"He's not worried about you. He won't commit because he's worried about me mating with an unknown third entity that might or might not be male."

"Ah."

She pushed her hair back from her face. "And I don't know how to make him change his mind."

Kaiden slid one hand behind his head and regarded her carefully. "Subterfuge? You said you could get me to Pavlovan, why can't you get Mac there as well in a less 'committed role'? Then if he meets your third, things might change."

6

Mac stripped off the now wet label of his second beer with his fingernail, conscientiously scraping off every bit of glue as he went. He hadn't even finished what was inside the bottle, his senses so attuned to what was going on with Neeve and Kaiden that he couldn't seem to coordinate swallowing beer and breathing.

He knew what he'd like to be swallowing right now...

And the fact that he was sitting here alone was entirely his own fault. He'd gotten so used to guarding every fucking thought that he'd forgotten how to be anything but a discarded super soldier and a second-rate human being. Seeing Professor Dean had only reinforced his determination not to let her get any emotional reaction from him ever again. She was the one who'd told him Leah had died, and recorded his total shock, his tears and his rage and then used them against him and the others to show how unstable he was when she'd decided to close the program.

Of *course* he'd threatened to fucking kill her. She'd known Leah was dying and prevented him from going to her simply to observe the 'reaction of human tragedy on a super soldier', or whatever her scientific paper had been called. And now she was here, sniffing around to see how he was reacting to a female telepath. He couldn't expose Neeve to that. He'd rather die.

A slight sound had him sitting upright and turning toward the kitchen. Neeve stood by the sink pouring a bottle of water into a glass. Her long auburn hair hung over one shoulder like a mermaid's.

"Hey." She nodded at him, but didn't come over.

His gaze took in her damp flushed skin and swollen mouth, the slight bruise at her throat and the way her robe clung to her thighs because she was wet from Kaiden's come. Without thinking, he rose to his feet and went toward her.

"I can't do this."

"Which part?" She remained calm, her glass of water in one hand, and the other on her hip.

"Sit here by myself."

"Then come back with me. It's a big bed."

"It's really that simple to you?"

"Yes. Mac, it is. I'm in need and I want you. Isn't that enough?"

And just like that all his carefully prepared arguments to protect her disappeared. His woman needed him, and there wasn't really anything he wanted more than to do what she asked him to. She wasn't Leah, she wasn't even from Earth and she'd already shown him that she was quite capable of defending herself.

He followed her down the short hallway and into the bedroom, shucking his clothes as he went. She waited until he was fully into the room and closed the door behind him. She put one finger to her lips.

"Wait. Security measures."

Her thoughts flew to him so much faster than anyone else's. He nodded as she casually placed her palm flat on the wall beneath the control panel. He actually staggered as a shot of her energy went through him leaving his mind feeling like half of it had been shut down.

"What did you do?"

"Closed off all security links to this space, why?"

He rubbed his head. "It feels like you turned off half my brain."

Kaiden sat up, his eyes widening. "Mac? I can barely sense you anymore."

"It's okay." Neeve said. "It's just a temporary block until we're either done with our mating, or your scientist finds a way around the new shielding protocol I introduced. *Can you hear me, Mac?*"

"*Loud and clear.*"

"*She obviously has done something to you.*" Neeve frowned. "*We can deal with that later. Are you still okay to mate?*"

Kaiden grinned. "His cock is."

Mac glanced down at his half-undone uniform pants and fumbled with the straining zipper to release the hungry thrust of his wet cock. With a low sound, Neeve sank to her knees in front of him and nuzzled his soaking boxers, licking and breathing in the scent of his arousal.

"*Mmm. I want this.*"

She helped him step out of his pants and underwear and then her mouth fastened around his shaft. She sucked him with long languorous pulls from root to tip that had him groaning and thrusting back at her.

"Slow down, I—"

She didn't listen to him, so he just lost himself in the pleasure of watching her lips parted around his cock as she sucked him dry. He didn't even put his hands on her, just let his cock slide back and forth as she dictated, his body and mind following along the salacious path of her imagination. Pressure built at the base of his spine and he knew he was close to coming.

She sensed it just as he did and moaned around his dick, increasing the draw on his flesh until he could hardly bear to move because the pressure and pleasure were so exquisite. He closed his eyes as the dark red of her thoughts rolled over him and surrendered. Each jet of his come was slow and languid and separately received down her willing throat.

Mac waited until she released his cock and then reached down to pick her up and sat her on the side of the bed. Knowing that Kaiden couldn't hear most of what he was saying telepathically was strangely liberating. He wondered what it was like in a true threesome when everyone heard each other so perfectly. It was kind of a terrifying thought but also deeply alluring. To have no secrets from two others...how did anyone deal with that?

"You don't have to share everything all the time. Even within a triad, your mind is your own and you are perfectly at liberty to set your own boundaries."

"Like not reading someone's mind when they aren't linking to you?"

She smiled. *"Yes. You really need to work on your shields."*

"So it's my fault?"

"Kind of." She shrugged drawing his attention to her breasts and tight pink nipples. *"You're the only person who can set your personal boundaries and then it's up to you to communicate them to others."*

He leaned in and licked her nipple swirling his tongue over the hardened bud until she shivered. He did it again, drawing more of her breast into his mouth until he was sucking her hard.

"Kaiden, can you keep her hands behind her back?" He practically had to shout to get the thought across.

"Sure." His commanding officer crawled over to the end of the bed and sat behind Neeve, his thighs framing hers, his chest

to her back. He drew her wrists back and wrapped one big hand around them both. *"Like this?"*

"Yeah."

Mac continued licking and sucking at her breasts, aware of her body moving easily between him and Kaiden. He took a quick look over Neeve's shoulder and saw how her ass was rubbing against Kaiden's dick with every undulation of her hips. Wetness gathered at the tip and slicked onto her skin making the glide even easier.

"That's good." Kaiden murmured, one big hand coming to rest on Neeve's jutting hipbone as he started to rock harder into the motion.

Mac kissed a long slow line down between Neeve's breasts over her flat stomach and fell to his knees. He buried his face in her mound. God, he'd missed her, missed the sexy scent between her thighs, the cream of her cunt, the throb of her clit...

"Mac...Please."

He paused long enough to grin up at her. "Oh no, we're taking this slow. I don't want to run out of come again."

"You actually ran out of come?" Kaiden said hoarsely. "That's—"

"Not pleasant, trust me on that."

Mac ducked his head back down and simply stared at Neeve's already swollen clit and labia. Leaning in, he delicately licked her, tasting her own sweet scent and the more masculine tang of Kaiden's come and sweat. He'd soon take care of that. Replacing the other male's scent with those from his own body was a priority until she smelled like his female again.

She moaned as he licked her and swirled his tongue over her slit and then her already wide opening, pushing his tongue inside her, letting his jaw and chin graze her most sensitive flesh. His heartbeat thudded through his own cock, making him so hard he knew he had to be inside her soon or he'd die. He curled his tongue over her clit in an endless figure of eight until she came hard against his lips shuddering with the pleasure of it.

"Lift her up for me, Kaiden." He only had to picture what he wanted to make Kaiden understand. Using his massive strength, his commander lifted Neeve until her feet were planted on his thighs and her ass was high against his chest.

Mac stood up and wrapped a hand around his cock easing it away from his stomach. Stepping between Kaiden's wide spread thighs, he slid inside Neeve's cunt, his hips pushing him deeper with every thrust until there was nowhere else to go. He took his time pulling in and out making every stroke as long and smooth as he could. Kaiden held Neeve steady, his body an unyielding frame against which she could do nothing but take Mac's cock for as long as he could give it to her.

She moaned his name and tried to angle her hips to lessen the impact of his thrusts. Kaiden held her tightly until Mac started to lose the battle and shortened his stroke his flesh slapping against her wetness and the swell of her hard little clit.

He came deep and stayed rigidly still enjoying every hot spasm of seed meeting the clench of her orgasm.

"Let me put my mouth on her." Kaiden murmured. "Like this."

Mac pulled out and Kaiden lifted her even higher until Neeve was kneeling on his broad shoulders and reaching for Mac to steady her against him. Kaiden ducked his head and started to lick Neeve's cunt. Mac couldn't take his eyes off the sight of Kaiden's tongue appearing through Neeve's slick folds, and eventually disappearing inside her.

Neeve's fingernails dug into Mac's shoulders as she started to writhe and shudder at the intimate contact. He cupped her breasts, worked her nipples in the same rhythm as Kaiden's agile tongue until she was gasping his name and coming. Her pleasure spilled into his mind and made him want to roar like some crazed cave man.

"My cock now."

Kaiden straightened and lowered Neeve down over his straining shaft. Mac went down on his knees in front of her and licked delicately at her clit until she screamed and started to move on Kaiden, using him to drive herself to another climax. Mac kept licking, his tongue sliding further back to circle where Kaiden impaled her, making his friend groan.

"Yeah, that's good, Mac, that's—"

Was this how it would feel to share another man? In the heat of mating, it didn't seem quite as terrible as Mac had imagined. But Kaiden was his friend, not some unknown Pavlovan who might decide to fuck his arse. He returned his attention to Neeve's clit until both she and Kaiden came and the three of them lay on the bed to catch their breath.

KAIDEN STRETCHED out his arms and groaned. "If that's what having a Pavlovan in your bed is like?" He bit Neeve's shoulder. "I want a Pavlovan."

"Not this one." Mac said.

"Noted Captain McNeill." Kaiden rolled over and got out of bed. "I need to eat something. I'll be back later."

Mac waited until Kaiden left the room before lying back down again.

"Why can't he have me?"

"You know why." Mac turned onto his side, kissed her knee and then her inner thigh. "He's not linked to you, like I am."

"How do you know?"

He found himself glaring up at her amused face. *Because I know. And you damn well know it too. Isn't that why we're trying to avoid each other?*

"I'm not trying to avoid you, Mac. I don't know how. You're the one with the issues. In my world, when a couple are obviously mated, you don't turn around and deny the link."

She didn't sound angry anymore, just sad and that made him feel like a heel.

"How can we be mated when we're from different cultures, different planets, and you'll be leaving in a few weeks? It makes no sense."

"I know." She touched his cheek. *"I wish I could consult the Oracle. She'd tell me what to do."*

"The Oracle's on Pavlovan, I assume."

"Yes." She hesitated. *"If I could get permission to leave this planet early and insist on taking a security detail with me, would you at least come and protect me until I got home?"*

"Go to Pavlovan with you?"

"Why not?" She searched his face and his mind. *"I could speak to the Oracle with you there. Then we would know if there was anything we could do about this situation."*

He thought about her leaving him and it made his heart ache.

"I don't know if Professor Dean would allow it."

Neeve raised an eyebrow. *"Professor Dean's influence does not extend to Pavlovan, I can assure you. If I ask to take you and anyone else I desire, my wish will be granted."*

Mac stared at her as an idea formed in his mind. "Do you mean that?"

"Yes."

He held out his hand. "Then I think we might have a deal."

THREE DAYS IN, and they were working well as a sexual team. Neeve felt fully provided for and was damn clear about expressing her desires. Having two tremendously fit super soldiers in her bed was almost as good as having two mated Pavlovan males. Tomorrow, she'd contact Pavlovan high command and ask if she might return early for her own safety. She had no doubt they'd agree. Her security was considered paramount to the existence of her nation. The fact that they'd even let her come to Earth was a minor miracle.

But until that happened, she intended to enjoy the last few hours of freedom with her two males. Shifting position, Neeve backed into Mac's half-erect cock. He murmured her name and drew her closer his shaft sliding between the cheeks of her ass. She was so wet and open now that he slid easily inside her cunt and slowly stroked back and forth.

Kaiden's hands settled on her breasts and played with her nipples.

"Fuck my ass, Mac. Let Kaiden in, too." Neeve ordered.

"Yes, ma'am." Mac slipped out of her and reached for the lube that sat on the side table. Not that she needed it much now. The two males had penetrated her so many times that she was wet enough to take them both wherever they wanted, but it never hurt to be careful.

Mac eased into her ass and then rolled onto his back holding onto her. He braced his feet on the bed and Neeve settled her legs within his, spreading her knees wide.

"Nice." Kaiden said.

He crawled toward them and knelt between their thighs. He was such a big man that his hips almost didn't make it. He slicked a hand over his shaft bringing it down toward Neeve and rubbing the crown against her clit until she moaned.

"Very nice."

He eased inside her, his thick cock swallowed up by her cunt inch by inch until he was fully inside her. Smiling, Kaiden took her hand and placed it over her clit.

"Help us out, here."

"As if you need it." Neeve tightened her internal muscles

until Kaiden groaned and Mac bucked against her ass. "I like this."

"Both of us?" Kaiden asked.

"Two cocks." She gently stroked her clit and shivered. "How does it feel to be so close to each other?"

"*Weird.*"

That was definitely Mac.

Kaiden looked more thoughtful. "It's very stimulating."

Mac snorted. "You mean you like it?"

"What's not to like?" Kaiden rolled his hips. "When I'm on top like this I can feel you both, I can make you both come."

Neeve settled more of her weight on Mac and his breathing hitched as she trailed her fingers downward pausing to circle Kaiden's cock and then even further back to stroke his taint. Kaiden started to rock forward, his hand braced on the side of the bed so that he could look down at his cock. Neeve reached up her free hand to cup his bristly cheek. Even his incoming beard was fair and hardly visible.

"*Would you let me try something, Kaiden?*"

"*Will it hurt?*"

"*No. My Second Male showed me how to do it. He loved it.*"

"*Then go ahead.*"

Neeve reached for the lube and slathered her finger in gloop. "*You can carry on.*"

"*Thank you.*"

"*Gently.*"

She sensed Mac watching her as closely as she brought her arm around Kaiden's hips and stroked her fingers down between the two flexing globes of his ass. He went still for a second and then resumed his slow thrusts as she rimmed the pucker of his ass with her slick finger until he started to push back against her as well as forward.

"*God...*" He breathed out hard as the tip of her finger penetrated him. "*That's...*"

She eased in a little further; fucking his ass to the rhythm he'd set. Then instinct took over as his pleasure roared through her and Mac and they became nothing more than an entangled rush of extreme sensations.

"More—give me more." Kaiden demanded. She slid a second finger in alongside the first. He bucked against her hand and hammered into her, pushing her onto Mac who held himself rigidly inside her ass. She screamed into Kaiden's shoulder and bit down hard as he climaxed taking her and Mac with him.

It took her a long time to open her eyes and tear herself away from the two men. Mac fell back onto the bed and Kaiden rolled onto his back, his chest heaving.

"Shower, I think."

Neeve let Mac pick her up and carry her into the stream of hot water where he washed them both clean. When she was finished, he returned with her to the bed and placed her carefully on the sheets.

"I'll be back in a minute."

She kept hold of his hand. "Are you okay?"

"Yes." he managed a smile. "Let me finish showering, and then I'll come back."

He returned to the bathroom and found Kaiden already in the shower. His commanding officer looked at him.

"Sorry, I thought you were done."

After a deep breath, Mac stepped into the shower and faced Kaiden. "What did it feel like?"

Kaiden rubbed at the water splashing off his massive chest. "You know what it was like. You got the whole telepathic sideshow."

"So you weren't faking for Neeve's benefit?"

"When I'm fucking a female who's being fucked by another

man and she's also finger fucking my ass, how the hell do you think I'd fake anything?" Kaiden licked his lips. "It was so damn hot."

Mac's cock twitched and he ran an absent hand over it. Kaiden was half-erect too.

"What about if a man did that to you? Would it feel the same?"

Kaiden's pale gaze met his. "I don't know. Are you offering?"

"You'd let me do that?"

"Why not?" He gaze dropped to Mac's clenched fist and then across to his cock. "Your fingers are thicker and longer than Neeve's. It could be even better."

"I—"

"You want to try it to see if you could stand having another male in your bed on a permanent basis." He nodded. "I understand. I told Neeve she could use my cock as much as she liked and I'm okay with you using my ass, too."

"Seriously, Commander?"

"Rank's not a problem here either, Mac. In this instance, we're just two males doing our best to understand and explore the Pavlovan sexual culture. I'm not going to run out and report you."

Kaiden turned the shower off and brushed past Mac, grabbing a towel on his way. He headed back into the bedroom and Mac followed him. Kaiden grabbed the lube and tossed it at Mac.

"Go ahead."

"Mac?" Neeve looked from him to Kaiden and then back again.

"Will you suck Kaiden's dick while I finger-fuck his arse?"

She nodded, swept her hair back over one shoulder and looked expectantly at him,

"Kaiden on your knees, Neeve in front of him and I'll..."

He glanced down at the lube and then at Kaiden's arse. He

was about to fuck his commanding officer's arse with his fingers. The thought of it, the thought of the three of them sharing the sensation made him so aroused he couldn't believe it. But he had to know if he could even contemplate sexually servicing another male. It was only fair to Neeve.

Neeve leaned in low and licked the crown of Kaiden's cock with the tip of her tongue. After three days, even after their most inventive efforts to stay hard, they were both quite sore and she obviously knew it. He crawled around to view the flex of Kaiden's hips as she drew him into her mouth, and the way his buttocks clenched and released.

The lube was warm on his fingers as he spread it over his index finger and stroked a line down from the end of Kaiden's spine to the tight circle of his arse. He tried to remember in his mind what Neeve had done and circled and played with Kaiden's puckered hole and the soft skin of his taint. From the way, Kaiden arched his back, almost presenting himself to Mac, he had succeeded in arousing him.

"Put it in me. Fuck me with that big thick finger, Mac." Kaiden's guttural command stirred something low in his belly. He pressed forward with the tip of his finger and felt Kaiden give into him and allow him past the tight ring of muscle.

"Yeah. Harder."

Mac obeyed, still mesmerized by the disappearance of his finger inside the other man. He pushed harder and was rewarded by a moan.

"God, that's deep, that's... Move it in and out of me, Mac."

Mac obliged and adapted his rhythm to Neeve's who had the whole of Kaiden's cock in her mouth and down her throat now. She looked beautiful to Mac, her eyes closed, her hair messed up by all their lovemaking and her nipples hard from being sucked and played with for three days straight. Her breasts swung gently as she sucked and he noticed she had one hand over her mound as she finger fucked herself.

"More."

Mac lubed up another finger and carefully eased it in alongside the other one. Kaiden cursed and rocked back on his heels as Mac pistoned his fingers back and forth scissoring them as wide as he could until Kaiden was screaming with pleasure in his head.

"All of them, Mac. Four fingers, I want—"

"Are you sure?"

"Goddamit, yes!"

Ignoring Kaiden's demand for him to hurry, Mac took his time until all four of his fingers were encased in Kaiden's arse. His own cock was hard and wet and pressed against Kaiden's hip. He couldn't help but move it in time to his finger thrusts and wonder what it would be like to be inside Kaiden, inside any man.

He started to slide his fingers in and out, pushing them as deep as he could and then almost out again. Along the way, Kaiden seemed to learn the trick of clenching his internal muscles to try and keep Mac deep. He soon forgot to be careful and slammed into him, each stroke like a fist as the immensity of Kaiden's pleasure thundered through his mind and through Neeve.

"God..." Kaiden went still and then he started to climax. Mac's cock joined him, jets of his come dripping down over Kaiden's hip and his still engaged fingers. As Neeve cried out too, Kaiden lurched for her and brought his mouth down onto her cunt licking and sucking her, his fingers buried deep until she climaxed again and again.

Mac managed to get off the bed and wash again, his legs felt wobbly and his mind was clouded. At the last moment, he'd wanted to pull out his fingers and shove his dick in Kaiden instead. He'd been so close to actually doing it. Had the others noticed? No one had said a word. If Kaiden had begged him, would he have obliged? He was no longer sure.

When he returned the other two were still where he'd left them, Kaiden's face was buried in Neeve's sex and he lay stretched out on the bed.

Neeve opened one eye as he approached. "I think I'm done."

"I think we all are."

A muffled groan from Kaiden confirmed his agreement.

"Let's try and make ourselves presentable before Professor Dean gets us into her lab. I don't think she's going to be very happy with me."

7

Mac glared at Professor Dean. "That fucking hurt."

"I'm taking a blood sample."

"Then let someone competent do it. Let a *machine* do it. I think you just enjoy stabbing me."

"If I do, that can hardly come as a surprise. You effectively blocked my data stream, and I want to know how."

Mac set his jaw as she yanked out the needle. "You promised not to snoop on our lovemaking, so I'd say we were even."

She swung around her cool blue eyes assessing. "*Lovemaking?*"

"Sex, then." *Shit.* Mac shrugged then wished he hadn't as his arm started bleeding again. "Whatever Pavlovans like to call it."

"How exactly did you block me from that apartment?"

He met her gaze. She was like a dog with a bone. "I didn't do anything."

"Then who did?"

"If Dr. Neeve wants to keep her sexual adventures quiet, I'm not going to argue with her." He offered up a half-truth. "She definitely did something. I felt my telepathic pathways freeze up."

"You did? How about Commander Kaiden?"

"I have no idea. I'm sure you've already spoken to him about it. My guess is that it's some Pavlovan protection barrier against outside interference with a mating session. It makes sense in a society full of telepaths who could listen in."

Professor Dean continued to stare at him before slowly returning her gaze to the vial of blood.

"Dr, Neeve returns to Pavlovan in a month."

"Yes."

"You'll service her once more and then your duty here will be over. I've requested your transfer to my lab."

Mac stood up and pulled on his uniform shirt. "And I've already put it on record that I will not accept that transfer."

"You might have no choice." She let her gaze roam over his torso. She'd never forgiven him for turning down her offer for a fuck. "I can't wait to get inside your head again.".

Mac picked up his pants and put them on. "Are we done here?"

"For now," Professor Dean nodded. "I'm not completely finished analyzing your results yet, so don't go far."

"Yes, ma'am." Mac saluted and walked out of the lab and back through the hallways to his own office. The thought of Professor Dean performing surgery on him made his flesh crawl. Even if Neeve couldn't follow through on her promise to take him to Pavlovan, he'd never allow himself to be used as a test subject again.

"What's up?"

Neeve picked up way too fast on his emotions these days. He let out his breath and sat in his chair. *"Nothing."*

"Did you find out how much data Professor Dean collected on you?"

He rubbed his upper arm. *"From her extremely unhappy face and the way she stabbed me with her needle, I'd assume she didn't get what she wanted."*

"That's good."

"Yeah, if you could only teach me and all the other human telepaths how to do that."

"You already can, Mac. We're linked." There was a slight pause. *"Can you communicate with the others?"*

"I've never tried it from up here. We don't tend to socialize much. The professor's experiments left us all in a fucking mess."

"I understand. If I am successful in my mission, you'll need to contact your associates and bring them together for our departure. I can help you boost your telepathic signal if necessary, as can Kaiden."

"When are you planning on doing that?"

"Speaking to my planet's head of assembly? As soon as he wakes up, which will be in about five minutes."

"Do you need help?"

"No, this is one thing I need to do by myself."

"Good luck."

A knock on the door had Mac breaking off contact and focusing his attention on the far more immediate problem of who was using up all the water allocation in the labs and what was to be done about it.

———

Neeve typed in her secret code to the private line of the head of the Pavlovan Assembly and waited until she was also able to connect telepathically. Being so far away from her home, she needed at least some boost from the messaging systems but she was hoped the network was as secure at the assembly could make it.

"Neeve."

She smiled. "Hey Ash. How are you?"

His slow smile warmed her soul. In the last year since finding his female, he'd changed dramatically. Okay, maybe only to those who knew him and his family intimately, but it was still a welcome change.

"I'm fine." He glanced over his shoulder. "Soreya and Esca are asleep next door so don't get too loud."

"As if I would." They smiled at each other in perfect understanding. Neither of them were known for their outgoing personalities. "I have a favor to ask you."

"Go ahead." He nodded and his long silver hair slid over his shoulder.

"This is a one hundred percent secure line, isn't it?"

"Yes." he frowned. "Why, is something wrong? We were informed that the Earth military had cracked down on Etruscan attacks and that you were perfectly safe."

"I want to come home early."

"You don't feel safe?"

"There's that, and then there's another matter. I want to bring some humans with me."

"Why?"

"They are telepaths."

He sat back. "You're sure about that?"

"Yes. I can't be more explicit at this point, but they all need to get away from this planet."

"You want me to offer them refugee status on Pavlovan?"

"Could you do that?"

"Of course. I've grown a lot more powerful within the assembly since my triad was completed. Soreya gave me a new source of telepathic power that no one else has." He hesitated. "As long as your family is okay with it. Have you spoken to your mother recently?"

"I don't talk to her, she talks to me—you know that. She has no concept of an actual conversation."

"Do you want me to go and see her?"

"Would you?"

"I wanted to speak to her anyway." His smile tightened. "Soreya is concerned about her inability to have a child."

"Then you should definitely speak to her." Neeve leaned in closer. "Could you make it soon? I'm worried about what's going to happen to these telepaths."

"I'll confirm as soon as I can." He raised his eyebrows. "It's really that important to you?"

"It might be. By the way, these are all military personnel. I'll be asking the authorities here if I can use them as security for the trip home. If it all works as planned, I'll need you to back me up on this."

"I'll do that." He smiled. "It will be good to have you home, Neeve."

She sighed. "That depends."

"On what?"

"What do you think?"

"You can't run away from your destiny, forever."

She signed off and spoke into the silence. "Yes, I bloody well can."

***

"This is most unusual, Dr. Neeve, most unusual."

Neeve smiled sympathetically at the Commander-in-Chief of Earth's military. "My family *is* rather protective of me, General Schaeffer. There isn't much I can do about that. I'm sorry for all the inconvenience. It's just that once they realized there were a few telepaths on Earth who could help secure my return to Pavlovan, they wouldn't settle for anyone else bringing me home."

"One wonders how they found out about them in the first place."

She opened her eyes wide. "I didn't realize it was a secret. When my family asked if my mating needs were being met, I was happy to share that you had exceeded my expectations by providing me with telepaths. My planet is very grateful, and *very* amenable to continuing to share our telepathic skills with your emerging youth."

Of course, all he cared about was the military applications of telepathy, like the Etruscans. But she wanted to give him the opportunity to at least pretend to respond positively to the Pavlovan assembly's demands.

"I've been instructed by my government to release the required personnel to you for this mission. They will meet you at the space port when you depart tomorrow morning."

Neeve smiled. "Thank you, General. I appreciate your support." She shook his hand and waited for him to leave, accompanied by his large entourage. She could only hope he'd take the obnoxious Professor Dean with him.

"WELL?"

Neeve smiled at Mac who was sitting on her bed, his hands clasped between his knees. He wore his usual black military uniform and had just had his hair cut so short it looked like bristles.

"Well what?"

"Are we leaving or not?"

She leaned back against the door and considered him. "Yes, we are. Ash has arranged it all just as I asked him."

"Who's Ash?"

"He's the head of the Pavlovan Assembly."

"A useful man to know."

She debated mentioning her mother but decided it was far too early in their relationship to dump that on him. "He is. I'm also very fond of him." She noted the slight tensing of his shoulders. "He's one of the most powerful telepaths I've ever known.

He's gorgeous to look at too, long silver hair and a body to die for."

He looked up at her. "I can't wait to meet him."

She moved closer until she was standing between his knees.

"He can't wait to meet you either."

"Did you tell him we were lovers?"

She cupped his chin. "No. I'd rather wait and share that in person."

"Will he object?"

"It depends whether he likes you or not." His jaw flexed beneath her fingers and she fought a smile. "He is a very powerful man. His good will is important to cultivate."

"Understood," he murmured, and turned his face until his mouth brushed her thumb. He kissed her knuckle and then licked it. "When are we leaving?"

"Tomorrow morning."

"And the other telepaths?"

"Are definitely coming with us."

He let out his breath. "I still can't believe this is going to happen the way we planned. Are you sure Professor Dean can't interfere?"

"Mac, I just spoke to General Schaeffer himself. He's okayed all the details. Between him, Ash and my mother, I don't think the prof stands a chance." She bent to kiss him. "Are you still okay about this?"

"About accompanying you to Pavlovan?" He met her gaze head on. "If it means I can save the other telepaths from becoming Professor Dean's lab rats, then yes."

She took a step backward. "So it's purely a business decision."

"You know it's more than that." He stood up. "I want to hear what this Oracle of yours has to say."

"And depending on what you hear, and how you interpret it, you'll decide whether to stay or go?"

"It's the best I can offer you at this point."

"For a telepath you are so damn unemotional." She turned on her heel, her heart a tight fist in her chest.

"Neeve—"

"What?" She wouldn't turn around.

"Give me a chance here, will you? I'm trying, I really am."

"Understood. Good night, Mac, see you at the spaceport at 0500 hours." She held the door open until he came toward her.

"Would you rather I lied to you?"

"Of course not."

He stopped in front of her and it took every centimeter of her control not to reach out and touch him. "I'm not trying to fuck you around, but—"

"I *know*. Just fucking's fine without all the other stuff. Go away."

She stepped around him, pushed him hard in the chest and shut the door in his face. The fact that he could enter her mind at will meant her action was pointless, but it was, at least, symbolic. It hurt her to realize he didn't understand her world as much as it hurt him to consider sharing her with anyone else.

Neeve sat down on the bed still warm from Mac's presence. Whatever the Oracle said, there were still a lot of issues to decide. Getting Mac to Pavlovan was only the first step of a potentially long battle. Would they ever see eye to eye?

8

WAKING UP FROM STASIS AND REUNITING WITH THE OTHER SIX members of the super soldier project who'd agreed to leave Earth was a surprisingly emotional experience for Mac. He hadn't expected to feel so in tune with them so fast. Apart from Neeve, the rest of the crew were unable to communicate telepathically which meant the telepaths could exchange information quickly and easily without having to worry about Professor Dean and her colleagues analyzing every thought anymore.

Some of the men were stronger telepaths than others, but the ease with which they slipped back into the same command structure was both surprising and reassuring. Kaiden was a natural leader and all the men automatically deferred to him. It was good to sit down and explain the situation in more detail, outlining the potential to stay in Pavlovan if they wished, and the likelihood of Professor Dean reclaiming them as research subjects if they did choose to return to Earth.

Mac sat back and watched everyone's faces as Kaiden outlined the mission ahead. Everyone except Declan O'Hara seemed enthusiastic about meeting other telepaths and exploring the possibilities of a new world. Mac knew that it wasn't because Declan didn't want to be there. It was more that he was always the last of the bunch to commit to anything. His caution had saved more than one of the super soldiers' lives, and his opinion, when given, was always respected.

"Do we have to remain in the military?" Declan finally asked.

Kaiden looked at Mac. "I don't think so, Dec, but we can confirm that with the Assembly leader when we arrive."

"Good."

That was all Declan had to say at this point. He nodded his auburn head and studied his clasped hands.

Kaiden stood up. "I think it's time you all met Dr. Neeve. She's the Pavlovan female who arranged for us to leave Earth. We'll be protecting her on the last stage of this journey to Pavlovan through potentially hostile space."

There was a knock on the door and Neeve came through. She seemed unfazed as all the males shot to their feet and saluted her. Having not seen her for several weeks himself, Mac drank in the sight of her braided auburn hair and the tight blue uniform that emphasized her tall curvaceous shape.

"*Put your tongue back in your mouth, Mac.*" Luckily, Kaiden sent the thought privately and Mac snapped back to attention.

"Commander Kaiden, Captain McNeill." She nodded at the rest of them. "I appreciate the escort back to Pavlovan. As I'm sure Kaiden has told you, we are approaching hostile space. I'm not expecting any trouble, but you never know with the Etruscans. They aren't even officially at war with our planet, but they do have a nasty habit of stopping our ships and exterminating telepaths. So we'll be taking a circuitous route to circumvent the more obvious trade routes and hopefully avoid any trouble."

Declan O'Hara saluted. "Excuse me, Dr. Neeve. Are you a telepath?"

"Yes." Neeve looked over at Declan and Mac found himself moving to stand between them.

"I thought so." His smile was very sweet. "Just checking, doc."

Neeve smiled at him. "All Pavlovans are born with some strain of telepathy. Some families tend to produce stronger telepaths than others and have accumulated power and wealth over the years. Developing your telepathic abilities is considered the most important thing a citizen can do to improve his or her life."

"Apart from mating."

Neeve's gaze flew to Mac's. *"I'm not going to get into that when I'm the only female aboard, okay?"*

"You're my female."

That possessive comment got him blocked so hard he almost winced.

Despite that, he went to stand beside her. "If any of you have any questions about what awaits us on Pavlovan, I'm sure Dr Neeve will be more than willing to answer them during the week ahead. But for now, let's pretend we're a unit again and concentrate on drawing up a strategic plan to secure this ship from the Etruscans."

"THIS DOESN'T LOOK GOOD." Kaiden muttered as he studied the view from beside the captain's chair. "Three Etruscan vessels are converging on us. Have they attempted to contact you?"

"Nothing yet." Captain Wertz scanned the navcom screen in front of him.

"Is it worth trying to communicate with them first?" Mac asked.

"I'd rather not draw any more attention to us. What do you think, Wertz?"

"To be honest, I've never been hailed or chased by an Etruscan ship before. I've heard they are relentless."

"Are there any Pavlovan ships in this sector?" Neeve sounded a lot calmer than the ship's captain, which was a blessing. "It might be worth trying to find some back up just in case."

"But if we start contacting Pavlovan ships, the Etruscans might see that as an act of aggression." Captain Wertz said. "Planet Earth has worked very hard to maintain our neutral stance in all these intergalactic squabbles."

"*Squabbles?*" Mac glared at the man. "You do realize that if we're boarded, we'll all be dead?"

"I thought they only took the telepaths."

"Captain, all the military personnel on this ship are telepaths. If you expect them to defend you and your crew, then you have to cooperate with us."

Neeve leaned forward and tapped the navcom. "There's a Pavlovan ship right here not too far to the left of us."

"I can't see it." Mac glanced down at the screen. "How can you tell?"

"It's shielded, but I can sense the telepaths on board. We're all using these routes to avoid the Etruscans at the moment. It stands to reason that someone would be out here."

"Can you communicate with them without using the ship's systems?"

"I'll have to." Neeve grimaced. "This ship doesn't have the capability. It also doesn't have great shielding, but that we can fix."

"Sir." Captain Wertz spoke in an undertone to Kaiden. "I am not authorized to allow modifications to this ship."

Kaiden clapped him hard on the shoulder. "That's okay because I am, and I have the approval of both governments to do whatever is necessary to get Dr, Neeve safely home to Pavlovan." He raised his voice. "Lieutenant O'Hara? Get up here." He smiled at Captain Wertz. "I'm officially relieving you of command of this vessel."

"But—"

"O'Hara, take the helm. Roberts take over at weapons."

The captain was politely but firmly escorted off the bridge. His protesting voice could still be heard as the doors shut behind him.

Neeve turned to Mac and Kaiden. "Can you two help me boost my signal?"

"Can we?" Mac asked.

"Tell your men to raise their shields first." Neeve added.

"Done." Kaiden moved closer. "Should we hold hands or something?"

"It's not necessary. Just attempt to blend your power with mine as I project this message."

Despite himself, Mac ended up holding her hand as he allowed his telepathic power to blend with hers and Kaiden's. The information shot from them at such high speed and volume that he felt the other telepaths shields start to buckle.

"*Damn.*" Kaiden groaned. "*That fucking hurt.*"

"It would be better if we had a complete triad. But they got the message loud and clear and are altering course to escort us."

Her smile grew as the Pavlovan military vessel drew closer and let down its shields. "We hit the jackpot. This is a class one military ship with a full complement of military personnel on board."

The main screen flickered and two faces appeared.

"Dr. Neeve, how good to see you again."

Mac found himself leaning closer to Neeve as she grinned at the two males. One of them was dark haired and huge, and the other was blond and sat in the captain's chair.

"Esca."

"Hey, beautiful." The darker man winked. "Ash sent us."

"That's great." Neeve said. "Are you going to escort us all the way?"

"That's affirmative." The blond nodded, his gaze shifting from Neeve to Mac. "Commander Kaiden? I'm Trenx, captain of this vessel."

KATE PEARCE

"No, I'm Captain McNeill." Mac drew Kaiden forward. "This is Kaiden."

"Good to meet you, sir." Both men nodded at Kaiden. "Do you need additional troops on board, or can you manage with the men you have?"

"We'll manage, Captain Trenx."

"Trenx will do fine. Hopefully when the Etruscans see that you aren't alone, they'll frek off back to their own planet."

"We can only hope." Kaiden replied. "We appreciate the support."

"Sir! The Etruscan ship is firing straight at us." Roberts shouted.

Even as O'Hara spoke the ship rocked, and alarms started to go off all over the bridge.

"Major damage to left forward engine, sir. Shutting it down and turning to auxiliary power." "O'Hara's voice remained a calm thread throughout the blaring alarms and flashing lights. "Etruscan ship is preparing to fire again. Hold on, I'm taking evasive action."

Trenx's voice sounded in Mac's ear through the interspaceship intercom. "Tell weapons to target sector three zee seven on the Etruscan ship. We'll do the same. It should take their weapon capability out. On my command…"

"Will do, sir." Roberts' hands flew over the sensor pads and there was a lurching sensation as they fired back. A bright flare from the Pavlovan ship met with theirs and the Etruscan ship peeled away.

"One down, two to go," Mac muttered. Neeve was running toward the central controls. "You shouldn't be up here."

The look she shot him was eloquently dismissive. "Then who else is going to get these crappy Earth shields up to scratch? I'm the only one with the technology."

"Tell me how to do it."

"I don't have time. How about you just shut up and help me?"

He vaulted over the command chair and joined her at the consul. The speed of their telepathic connection meant she could relay the information and he could implement it without losing a second.

"Shit." Kaiden muttered as a second volley hit the ship. "Where the hell did that come from?"

"Engine three is out, sir." Robert's shouted.

"We're on it." Trenx again. "Taken out. Commander Kaiden, we suggest immediate evacuation. We are far more capable of protecting you, Neeve and the Earth crew on our ship and getting you home quickly."

Kaiden looked over at Mac and Neeve. "Agreed."

"We'll send over our shuttles. We should be able to take you all in one hit."

"Don't say hit."

Trenx's laughter rang through the com system. "Over and out."

"Esca!"

Neevie!"

She leapt straight into the arms of the tall dark-haired Pavlovan soldier and allowed him to pick her up and swing her around in a giant hug. Mac and Kaiden waited until the man put her down again, Kaiden looked more amused than Mac felt.

The sensation of telepathic thoughts all around him was amazing and unsettling at the same time. The ship hummed with it like an overactive hive. He could only hope his shields were good enough to keep most of the background noise out.

Still holding the Pavlovan's hand, Neeve turned to him and Kaiden.

"I'm sorry, it's been a while since I've seen this idiot.

Commander Kaiden, Captain McNeill, this is Esca, Ash's Second Male."

Mac stared at the rugged soldier. This guy was the second male in a triad? He didn't look like he'd be willing to take second place at anything or to anybody. He saluted and then found his hand being grabbed and shaken in a hard grasp.

"Captain McNeill. Thanks for bringing our precious cargo home safely."

Neeve rolled her eyes. "Precious, me?" She seemed so much more alive with Esca that, for a second, Mac wondered why she'd bothered to bring him back at all. He dismissed that thought as Esca led them through the decks, talking as he went and pointing out various places of interest. Eventually he stopped and punched a code into one of the doors and then the one next to it.

"We're a bit tight on space at the moment, so I hope you don't mind sharing. Neeve you're in here. Commander Kaiden and Captain McNeill are next door."

Mac stepped forward. "I'll share with Dr. Neeve."

Esca looked at him. "There's no need. This ship is one hundred percent secure."

Mac turned to Neeve. "Do you want me to stay with you?"

"Even if I say no, you'll turn up at some point, won't you?"

"If you need me, yes, but if you'd rather I shared with Kaiden that's fine with me."

"Am I missing something, here?" Esca asked.

Just as Mac said yes, Neeve said no.

Kaiden chuckled. "As you can see. It's complicated." He shifted his bag over his shoulder. "I'm going next door. Call me if you need a referee."

Esca lingered, his interested gaze flicking between Neeve and Mac. "Captain McNeill's a telepath, right?"

"Yes." Neeve went into the room and Mac followed her.

"Are you sure—?"

Mac shut the door in Esca's face and leaned against it. Neeve walked through to the tiny attached bathroom and slammed that door hard. He sighed. Within a few minutes she came back, minus her uniform, in a matching bra and panty set and glared at him. He studied her luscious curves and hoped he really wasn't drooling.

"I missed you."

She raised one eyebrow. "So?"

"I'd like to make love to you."

"Not just fuck me?"

"Well, I suspect my first effort might be a five second fuck because I'm so desperate, but after that, I hope to satisfy you all night."

He took a tentative step forward and then another until he could reach out and slide his fingers into her hair. She closed her eyes and leaned toward him with a soft sound that made him want to wrap his arms around her and hold her close forever.

"I don't like feeling this way, Mac." Her voice was muffled against his chest.

"What way?"

"Wanting you when you're not committed to me."

"I'm here, aren't I?"

She slowly raised her head and looked up at him. "I suppose you are."

"So how about we make the best of it?"

She slid a hand between them and grasped the heavy thrust of his cock through his pants.

"I wish I could say no."

He forced himself to stay still. "You can always do that. I'll never force you. If you can't deal with me, I'll go and share with Kaiden. I mean it."

"Is that a threat?"

"No, I know you're not happy with this situation and I don't want to make things worse. If not sleeping with me makes it easier for you, then I'll respect your decision."

"You mean it don't you?"

His dick yelled no, but he nodded anyway.

"So we just make the best of it?"

Her fingers slid away from his cock and he wanted to cry. Just as he went to take a step back she unbuttoned his pants and worked the zipper down. And then it was all over for him. Within another second, he had her on her back on the bed and he was moving between her legs. He pulled off her panties and cupped her mound groaning at the flood of wetness that filled his palm.

"*Damn.*"

He wrapped one hand around his cock and pushed himself deep inside her welcoming, hot cunt. He'd barely managed a single thrust before she started to come. He fucked her so hard his vision blurred into a red cloud of lust and emotion that made remembering to breathe his primary objective for quite a while.

He managed to roll onto his back and she crawled over him and just lay there panting alongside him.

"God, I forgot about shielding my thoughts." Mac groaned. "Did I just broadcast that entire experience to the whole ship?"

"All ten seconds of it?"

"Better than I expected."

"It's okay, I shielded for us both. Most telepaths are used to having to block the odd uncensored scream of pleasure from a mating couple."

He leaned up on one elbow and studied her beautiful face. "So what would it take to make you forget to shield?"

She fluttered her eyelashes at him. "Why don't you find out?"

He started undressing her properly admiring every inch of her creamy skin as it appeared, the soft curve of her breast and the delicious pink tips of her breasts that demanded his complete and utter attention.

He smiled as she tugged at his uniform shirt. "I don't think that's going to be a problem."

———

"So, Captain McNeill."

"What about him?" Neeve looked over at Esca who sat at his ease on the couch in the officer's mess. He'd changed into a tight black T-shirt and military issue shorts.

"He's a strong telepath."

"Yes, he is."

"Who obviously knows how to make you scream."

Neeve scowled at him. "You heard that? Damn."

"Darlin' the whole ship heard it. The engines went off line and we almost plummeted to our deaths."

"Exaggerator."

"Sure, but what gives?"

"It's complicated."

"Isn't it always?" He crossed his big bare feet at the ankle. "Look at how long it took me and Ash and Soreya to sort ourselves out."

Neeve looked around, but there was no one else there to overhear her confidences.

"It doesn't make sense. I've already loved and lost Malke. How could I possibly find a mate who isn't a Pavlovan?"

Esca shrugged. "I did. Soreya's Etruscan. Imagine how unbelievable that felt."

"But at least she agreed to come back with you to Pavlovan and work things out."

"Um, actually, she didn't. It was come to Pavlovan or extermination and even then, she didn't make the decision easily. Did the good captain come to Pavlovan for you?"

"He said he wanted to safeguard the future of his fellow super soldiers and agreed to come if I could bring them all."

"An honorable man."

"Yes, but I wanted him to want to come for *me*." Neeve felt like stamping her foot and sulking like a three-year-old.

"Maybe this was his way of achieving that, without actually admitting it?"

"I suppose that's possible. Males are peculiar about the emotional stuff."

"Do you really think Captain McNeill is your mate?"

"Yes, but he doesn't have a clue what that entails. Or should I say, he *does,* and the idea of being part of a triad scares the crap out of him."

"It scared Soreya, too."

"So what did you do about it?"

"We gave her time to make her own choices and then followed it up with the most fantastic sex any female was ever going to get in her life." He winked. "Best for us, too."

"You're so conceited."

His smile dimmed. "Yeah, I am, but it is fundamental to our existence as a triad. In order to bond mentally and emotionally, we have to bond physically."

"I *know.*"

"So what's the problem? From the sound of it you and the good captain have the physical part all sewn up."

"That's not the problem. It's adding a third."

"He doesn't share well?"

"It's not part of Earth culture to form triads. Especially if two of those members are men."

"Ah, I get it now. Do you want me to talk to him? Tell him how angry I was at getting paired off with Ash and being classed as Second Male?" He smiled. "Tell him how unbelievably wrong I was and that Ash fucking me is awesome?"

She reached over to pat his knee. "Let's see how things go with the Oracle first, but I might need your help after that."

"You've got it." Esca looked behind her. "Commander Kaiden, come on in."

"Call me Kaiden."

Neeve turned to smile at him and patted the couch beside her. "Did you sleep okay?"

He raised an eyebrow at her. "There were a couple of…interruptions but I did get some rest, thank you."

Esca snorted. "Oh yeah, poor you, you were right next door. "

"It wasn't a problem." Kaiden sat down. "How long before we reach Pavlovan?"

"Not that long now. Around twenty-four of your Earth hours."

Neeve got up and brought Kaiden a drink from the cold box. "Try this Pavlovan beer. It's supposed to be pretty similar to that brewed on Earth."

"Thanks."

Trenx came through the door and paused as he surveyed the group. "All's secure. We've outrun the Etruscan ships and we're just entering Pavlovan space. Any more of that beer?"

"At least six more that I could see," Neeve answered him.

Trenx took out a bottle, popped the cap and came around to sit down, shoving Esca's feet onto the floor.

"This is an interesting ship, captain."

Kaiden's slow voice had Trenx looking over at him.

"Thanks. It's loaded with weaponry and it's damn fast, which is good enough for me."

"And for us. If it hadn't have been for your appearance in Etruscan space, we might not have made it to Pavlovan."

Trenx raised his beer in the commander's direction. "You're welcome. If we have time, I'll show you round properly."

"I'd appreciate that." Kaiden drank slowly from his frosty bottle, his gaze remaining on the space ship captain.

Neeve knew him well enough to sense when something was of interest to him and, in this case, it was clearly Trenx. She also noticed that Trenx's gaze kept straying back to the big blond man who sat quietly drinking his beer as Esca rattled on about the latest news from Pavlovan.

"Why don't you show Commander Kaiden around the ship before dinner, Trenx?" Neeve asked. "I need to go and wake Captain McNeill, so you have time."

Kaiden put down his empty beer. "There's no hurry, Neeve. I'm sure Captain Trenx is a busy man."

Trenx stood up. "No, I'd like to show you around. You're also qualified as a pilot aren't you?"

"Among other things."

"Then it would be a good idea to give you a working knowledge of this ship in case I finally strangle Esca and you have to take command."

Kaiden's slow smile was met and returned by Trenx. "I'd be delighted to help out."

Esca turned to Neeve as the two men went out together.

"I take it Commander Kaiden doesn't have the same issues that your mate has?"

"He's certainly open to new experiences."

"I think Trenx likes him. I've never seen him be so polite before."

"Well, I think the feeling is mutual." Neeve stood up. "And I'd really better go and wake Mac up before dinner."

Esca waved at her. "Take your time. I'll wait."

9

Apart from one extraordinary difference, the Pavlovan spaceport was similar to all the others Mac had visited over his years in the military. The vibration of telepathic thoughts was like eavesdropping on a million connected minds and was quite overwhelming. All the super soldiers stopped walking and simply stood and gazed around them.

"I suggest everyone raises their shields until we get used to this." Mac said.

"Damn," whispered Declan. "That's amazing."

Mac waited as Esca and Trenx moved in front of Neeve leaving her protected on all sides. From the look on her face, she didn't appreciate the effort. He hardly had time to wonder why before they were moving off down the gangplank and into the reception area to the right of the landing bay.

What appeared to be a welcome committee awaited them. Esca was already grinning at someone in the lineup, so it was highly likely that Ash, the head of the Pavlovan Assembly and Esca's First Male was present. After meeting Esca, he couldn't help but wonder what Ash was like and how the two men lived with each other. He couldn't imagine anyone subduing Esca's primal fighting instincts.

"Oh *heeze.*"

Neeve whispered the words but Mac caught them.

"What's wrong?"

"Don't do that! She'll catch it and—"

The procession came to a halt and a slender man with long silver hair dressed in a flowing white suit stepped forward.

"Welcome to Pavlovan. The Assembly would like to extend our thanks to you for bringing First Daughter Neeve safely home. We would also like to offer you our protection and citizenship of our great nation if you choose to accept it."

Kaiden saluted. "Thank you. We are very grateful for the offer."

Mac studied the slight silver-haired male who emanated such strong psychic power that it positively radiated out of him. The man caught his gaze and smiled.

"I'm Ash. You must be Captain McNeill."

Mac saluted as Esca stepped out of line and went to kneel before Ash.

"First Male." He took Ash's hand and kissed it while Ash touched the top of his head.

"Second. I am glad to see you home safely once more."

Mac was about to turn back to Neeve when he noticed Esca's tongue sneak out and lick the seam where Ash's pants covered his dick. He hurriedly looked away, but not before Ash's hand clenched hard in Esca's hair.

"Neeve?"

A woman spoke from behind him and he automatically stepped out of the way. God, she was one of the most beautiful women he'd ever seen. Her hair was a glossy red, her eyes green, and her body perfection.

"Aleya. How are you?"

ALEYA RUSHED UP to Neeve and gathered her in her arms. "I'm so pleased to see you! I'm so sorry about Malke, we're all so sorry, we prayed for you."

"Thank you." Neeve tried to ease out of Aleya's embrace. "It was horrible to lose him."

Aleya still clung onto her hands. "We understand." She turned to Mac. "He is *the one?*"

Neeve looked anywhere but at Mac, who was happily gawping at Aleya's beautiful face. "We should get moving. It's cold out here. Esca and Ash have offered to put us up at their apartment until we make more formal arrangements."

"But, aren't you coming home?" Aleya pressed a hand to her breast. "We've all been expecting you!"

"I haven't lived at home for years, and I have no intention of returning there at present." Neeve forced a smile. "I do intend to visit you all soon and catch up, but I'm sure you'll understand that I have other duties."

"Oh, well, if you're sure." Aleya stepped back her pretty face a mask of confusion.

Neeve kissed her on the cheek. "I do appreciate you coming to welcome me home. It means a lot."

"Then I'm glad I came. We all wanted to come, but mother said it would be too overwhelming for you." She smiled at Mac. "I'm so glad you found each other. It's quite romantic isn't it?"

Neeve briefly closed her eyes. "Please don't make assumptions about anything yet, and if you can't help yourself then please, for all our sakes, keep them to yourself." She picked up her bag and slung it over her shoulder. "Captain McNeill?"

Mac followed her out of the reception area and into a slate black vehicle the size of a small planet where Kaiden and the other men were already seated. He took the seat next to her and waited until they'd moved off to raise his shields and hopefully cut everyone else out of the conversation.

"Who was she?"

"My sister, Aleya."

"Why didn't you want to go home with her?"

"I'm hardly going to arrive and leave you all to fend for yourselves, now am I?"

"I'm fairly certain Esca and Ash could cope. What's wrong?"

"It's complicated." She hunched her shoulder and looked out of the window at the shining silver buildings that lined the roadside. *"Can we talk about it later?"*

"If you will talk about it."

"Trust me," she offered him a small smile. *"I don't have a choice."*

Ash's home was huge and covered two floors containing six different suites of rooms. Ash had excused himself and gone back to work leaving the soldiers to sort out their room assignments on the lower floor. Neeve was offered a suite on the top floor, which Esca said had previously belonged to Soreya before she'd committed herself to moving in fully with Ash and him.

Mac dumped his kit alongside Neeve's and no one said a thing. Even she couldn't be bothered to argue about it right now. And it was probably better if he was alone with her when she had to tell him about her mother and the prophecies and all the other crap that had made her and Malke run as far away from Pavlovan as they could get. Everyone else disappeared to get settled, leaving her alone with Mac in the large modern white suite.

She started as his hand curved around her neck and he rubbed his thumb against the roundness of her spine.

"You're tense."

"There are good reasons for that."

"I thought you wanted to come home?"

"I don't think I had a choice." She sighed. *"I also wanted to make*

sure you and the others got away from such an invalidating environment."

"You mean Earth?"

"Professor Dean's treatment of you was barbaric."

His thumb stopped caressing her and he slipped in real speech. "I know. She treated us like lab rats for her own personal glorification. Is there a shower in here?"

She wasn't the only one who had difficulty in opening up about the past. Neeve pointed toward the second door. "The bathrooms through there."

He linked his fingers through hers. "Come on."

"But—"

"Just come and shower with me. You can tell me what's on your mind later."

She squeezed his hand. "Is it that obvious?"

"Only to me." He kissed her on the forehead. "I can read you so easily these days."

She followed him into the vast bathroom that Chase, Ash's housekeeper, always kept stocked with shampoo and lotions and anything else that an unexpected guest, let alone ten, might require during their stay. Neeve reckoned that if she asked, Chase would probably produce a complete wardrobe for her, too.

With a grateful sigh, she unzipped her space suit and put the massive shower on. As she undressed, she got the pleasure of watching Mac strip and enjoyed that immensely. Even though she'd seen him naked on the ship, the close quarters hadn't allowed her to really appreciate the sight of his tight abs, muscled shoulders and the way his body flexed and moved like an athlete's.

"What's wrong?"

He dropped his underpants onto the carpet and turned toward her. Her gaze immediately dropped to the dark hair at his groin and the growing thrust of his cock.

"Nothing. I'm just appreciating the view."

"As am I."

He smiled slowly, his dark blue gaze scanning her in return. Her nipples tightened and she felt a stirring of warmth low in her sex as his shaft grew even bigger. She walked with him into the shower, aware of the scent of her arousal rising around her and the wetness gleaming on the crown of his cock as it nudged her ass.

"Turn around."

She allowed him to maneuver her under the spray of the water and stood patiently as he soaped up his hands and ran them all over her skin until she was humming her satisfaction against his chest. It seemed natural to return the favor, so she washed him as well, paying particular attention to his balls and cock and the hard muscles of his ass.

"Mmm…nice," she whispered and looked down to where his shaft hotly throbbed against her belly. "But this definitely needs more washing." She went down on her knees and took him into her mouth sucking in both the faint remnants of soap and the far earthier tang of his pre-cum that continued to coat the crown of his cock.

Reaching between his legs, she cupped his balls in her palm and slid one finger up to stroke the soft skin of his taint. He started to move with her, his hips angling him forward into her mouth so that she had no choice but to take him deeper.

She circled the pucker of his ass with her finger until he was shuddering. With a groan, he slid a hand into her wet hair and cradled her skull.

"*Put it in me.*"

"*My finger?*"

"*Yeah, in my arse.*"

She gathered some soap on her finger and returned to her task circling and playing with his asshole until she could just wedge the tip of her finger inside him.

"God..."

He thickened even more in her mouth, his thrusts becoming shorter and more demanding as he arched his spine against the intrusion. She eased a little deeper and he bucked against her and started to come in thick hot waves down her throat, holding her head within his grasp so that even if she'd wanted to move away, she wouldn't have been able to.

As soon as he'd finished coming, he picked her up and walked through to the bedroom kicking open the door and bouncing her down onto the middle of the bed.

He was on her before she gathered her breath, his mouth sucking and licking at her breasts as his hands shaped her hips and ass and then centered on her sex. He drew back to stare down at her wide open legs, using his thumbs to spread the lips of her sex and then plunged both of them inside her in a demanding rhythm as his mouth descended on her clit.

"Mac, gods, I'm..."

She didn't need the words because she was too busy coming and grinding her sex against his stabbing and nuzzling tongue as he drew her even higher. He growled against her most tender flesh and moved again, his cock now sliding inside her. With a moan, she wrapped her legs high around his hips and dug her heels into his ass as he slowly pumped back and forth.

She came again and he slid his hands under her buttocks bringing her deeper into the thrust of his shaft and the grind of his pelvic bone against her most sensitive parts. His mind reached for hers and she opened to him on every level, let her pleasure echo in his mind and experienced his in hers.

"Don't be sad."

His words rang in her head.

"I'm not, I just wish...wish you were really mine."

She couldn't stop the thought and felt it smack against his fast rising shields. She shoved her hands between them and pushed on his chest.

"I can't do this anymore. Give you everything while you try and hide from me." She glared at him aware she was close to tears and hating the weakness of it. She shoved him hard until he gave her enough space to slide out from under him and scuttle to the corner of the bed.

"Neeve—"

She held up her hand. "Shut up! I know what you are going to say and I know I agreed we could just do the sex part, but I *can't*. It just doesn't feel right not to have that connection with you."

"But you fucked Kaiden."

"Because he and I both knew there was nothing between us. This…" she waved her hand at him "is completely different and it feels all wrong, as if you are deliberately ignoring what you know to be true."

Mac folded his arms across his chest and glared right back at her. "But I *don't* know it to be true. It is completely outside my experience of how a relationship is supposed to work. We don't do this shit on Earth!"

"You're not *on* Earth!"

He raised an eyebrow and her hand curled into a fist.

"Neeve, I agreed to come to Pavlovan with you, meet the Oracle and take it from there. If your Oracle says I'm destined to be your mate, then I'll accept it." He paused. "What's so impossible to understand about my thought process?"

"You'll *accept* it?"

His mouth curved up at the corner. "Do you think I'm stupid or something?"

"But what about our third?"

He shrugged. "I'll have to deal with that when or if it happens. Trenx told me I might have been you and Malke's third. If that's the case, there might not be another person to worry about."

Neeve stared at him for a long moment. "It's that simple?"

"It is if you want it to be." He paused and rubbed a hand over his scalp. "I know I'm not exactly what you expected Neeve, I've already picked up a lot of 'thoughts' about my unsuitability for you."

"From where?"

"There are millions of telepaths on Pavlovan. As you keep telling me, my shields need work. I'm already getting the sense that you're a princess and I'm an ignorant alien peasant."

She raised her chin. "No one's said anything to me. Ash approves and that's all that matters." That wasn't quite true, but she'd handle that when it happened.

He smiled and held out his hand. "Then will you come here and finish this?" He glanced down at his still hard cock. "And then you can tell me why you don't want to see your sister."

MAC GLANCED BACK at the bed where Neeve was sleeping. He walked over and drew the covers over her naked form, smoothing her long red hair away from her face. In sleep, her features looked more like her sister's than when she was in motion. He still hadn't gotten her to talk about what else was bothering her. Why did females have to make everything so damned complicated? Her outburst about his lack of "bonding" had been a sidetrack and once he'd explained his obvious reasoning, she'd had no option but to back down.

He pulled on a pair of boxers and a dressing gown that he found hanging in the bathroom. Perhaps he should've made her talk to him before they'd made love again and she'd fallen asleep. His stomach growled. But maybe it would be better to hear whatever was really wrong on a full stomach.

He left the suite and headed for the main family room and kitchen area, hoping that Chase would offer to make him a sandwich or something. He didn't even know the time, or how long a Pavlovan day was. The murmur of voices made him slow down, but it was too late to go back. The couple embracing in the kitchen had already seen him.

"Mac!" Esca called out. "Come and meet Soreya, our one and only female." He kept a casual arm around the petite female next to him.

"Captain McNeill."

Her accent was different to the Pavlovans and the brush of her mind against his was distinctly original.

"Please, call me Mac. And thank you for allowing us all to invade your home."

She shrugged. "I served in the Etruscan military. I'm used to being surrounded by soldiers."

"You're Etruscan?"

"By birth." She glanced up at Esca. "Any Etruscan male who shows signs of being telepathic is neutralized, but some of the females are kept to serve the army. That's how Esca and I met."

"I saved her life." Esca said and winced as his mate elbowed him in the gut.

"Actually, that's true, but I saved him first."

Mac couldn't help but smile as Soreya handed him a cup of real Earth-style coffee and something that resembled a square donut.

"Dinners going to be ready soon. But Chase spent all morning researching Earth food and that snack, whatever it is, should apparently keep you going. " She gestured at the couch. "Come and sit with us."

Mac followed her and Esca to the white couches in front of the floor to ceiling windows. The city scrolled out beneath them, the lights of the coast and the spaceport a twinkling array in the far distance.

"That's some view."

"I know. I couldn't believe it when Esca first brought me

here. I was so intimidated, but this is nothing compared to Neeve's home, I suppose."

Mac sipped at his coffee, which was strong, black, and just how he liked it. "I have no idea what Neeve's house looks like. I didn't even know she had one. Did she live in it with Malke?"

"Oh, I meant her family home. She'll probably take you there to meet her siblings at some point." Soreya paused as if Esca was communicating with her. "That is, if you are really mated."

"That's for the Oracle to say."

"That should be interesting," Esca murmured.

"Why?"

"Because the Oracle doesn't always say what you want to hear. I nearly threatened her with violence when she announced I was Second Male." He shook his head. "You don't do that to the Oracle. My parents nearly had a heart attack."

"You were quite young," Soreya patted his knee.

"Yeah, eighteen isn't the ideal time to find out you're going to be permanently on your knees sucking your First Male's dick." Esca grinned. "And then I met Ash and he let me go and do what I had to do, and then showed me just how much I was going to love sucking his dick."

"Esca!" Soreya slapped him this time and Mac fought a smile. "You're supposed to be reassuring Mac, not making things worse!"

"It's okay." Mac put his coffee down. "The whole concept of a threesome isn't one I'm used to on Earth, but seeing you guys together makes sense."

"I wasn't sure about it either." Soreya confessed. "But—"

"But when she realized she got me *and* Ash, she came around." Esca winked at his mate. "She came…a lot actually."

Soreya's cheeks were now red but she kissed Esca's chin. "My Etruscan family thought it was a sin for me to mate with another telepath, let alone two. I'm no longer considered part of their family, and I'm okay with that."

"Okay with what?"

Ash had come through the door. He dropped his case on the floor and advanced into the room shucking off his jacket as he went. Mac watched as Esca and Soreya turned to him like he was a fucking rock star. Even Mac felt his power. It changed the whole dynamic of the psychic space.

"Captain McNeill, how are you?"

Ash smiled at him as he came to sit on the couch next to Soreya. He dropped a kiss on Esca's cheek and then on the top of his female's head.

"Please, call me Mac. And thanks for putting us up. It's much appreciated."

"Neeve is my cousin. This is the least I could do to help her out. If your unit decides to stay on Pavlovan, we can provide you with accommodation and employment. Soreya works at the university where she teaches her extraordinary telepathic skill set to our youth. I'm sure you have additional skills we could learn from as well."

"I'm not sure about that. We were selected for having emerging telepathic traits and biogenetically engineered to enhance those abilities along with physical strength. We had to work damn hard to achieve everything."

"Which is a new concept for us. If you are willing, and only if you are willing, you could help our research scientists quite considerably. Ninety-nine percent of our population is born with some telepathic ability, which is nurtured from birth, but can also be taken for granted. Being able to offer opportunities to enhance that ability in different ways would be very useful."

When Ash smiled at him, Mac had to smile back. In fact, he wanted to crawl off the couch and go over and put his head right in Ash's lap and simply soak up his telepathic aura...

Esca snorted. "Stop it, Ash. You're making Mac uncomfortable."

"No, he's not, I'm just..." Mac tried to think of the right words. "It's like I want to—"

"Do this?"

Ash's beautiful mind flowed around his and he instinctively let him in and simply wallowed in the power of the exchange.

"Yes."

His cock jerked against his boxers fighting to get free. Ash gently broke away from his mind leaving Mac feeling like he'd just had the best orgasm of his life.

"Don't worry, Mac, I'm not jealous. Ash has that effect on people sometimes."

Mac jerked his head around to see Neeve coming through the bedroom door. She didn't seem too bothered to see him sitting there with a hard-on panting over her cousin.

Mac cleared his throat as Neeve sat down beside him and rapidly changed the subject. "Have the others settled in okay, Esca?"

"Yes, they are all coming up here for dinner, so you can check in with them then. Kaiden's got them all in hand."

"Good." Mac tried to ignore the way Neeve's hand had come to rest on his thigh. He wanted to grab her wrist and press her fingers firmly over his cock.

"You like an audience now?"

He glanced over at the others but no one seemed to have heard her remark as they discussed the upcoming dinner and where everyone was going to sit.

"No. If you did touch me right now, I'd probably come."

"You'd like Ash to see that, wouldn't you?"

Her fingers slid up his thigh, her thumb edging close to his balls and he caught his breath.

Her laughter echoed inside his head. *"I'm just kidding. Ash really can't help it. Telepathic charisma is a lethal weapon and he has it in spades. After you've spoken to the diplomatic liaison tomorrow, would you like to come and visit my family home?"*

"*If that's what you want.*"

She grimaced. "*It has to be done.*" The doorbell rang. "That will be Trenx. Hadn't you better go and get dressed?"

Mac glanced down at his dressing gown and the thick thrust of his cock. "*Only if you come and help me choose something to wear.*"

"*Like your uniform? You don't even have anything else, do you?*" She rose gracefully to her feet and held out her hand. "*You're on.*"

He followed her into their suite and shut the door, one hand already wrapped around his aching wet shaft. She immediately went down on her knees.

"Let me take care of that for you."

"I won't last more than ten seconds." Even while he protested he was shoving down his boxers and reaching for her. "*God...*"

She sucked him hard and fast as he imagined a man might do and he started to come at the thought of Ash watching him, fucking him, *owning* him…

Perhaps having a third person in your bed didn't have to be quite as alarming as he'd previously imagined. Luckily for him, Ash was already taken.

10

"*HEEZE*," NEEVE MUTTERED AS SHE LOOKED AROUND THE GILDED entrance hall. "I don't think she's here after all."

"Er, Neeve."

She turned to look at Mac who was staring up the stairs, his mouth open. "Who are all these women?"

She checked out the six or seven women who were running down the stairs toward them. "Them? Mainly my sisters and some of them are cousins."

"You have good genes in your family."

"Or you could say my mother picks great partners." She braced herself for the impact of a tidal wave of loving concern. "Hi siblings and cousins. This is Captain McNeill. He's mine, so don't touch him. Is our mother here?"

Sylvia stepped forward and threw her arms around Neeve. "It's so good to see you! I've missed you. We've all missed you."

"So Aleya told me." She forced herself to relax her shields a little. "It's good to see you all, but where is she?"

"Mother's at the sacred place. It's the festival of life week." Sylvia tugged on Neeve's arm. "But aren't you going to come in and visit with us? I'm sure we'd all love to hear what you've been up to and how you met Captain McNeill."

"I'm sorry, Sylvia, but I'm three days away from a mating meltdown, and I really need to speak to mother."

"Oh, I understand." Sylvia smiled again. "Perhaps you'll come by when you've seen her.

Neeve held onto her youngest sister's hand. "I'm sorry, I really mean it."

"It's all right. Duty must come before pleasure."

"Exactly." That wasn't what Neeve meant at all, but if it worked for her female relatives then she'd go for it. She grabbed Mac's hand.

"Put your tongue back in your mouth, and let's go."

He obediently followed her out and back into the limo Ash had lent her.

"Why didn't you mention that you grew up in a palace?"

"Why do you think?"

"You weren't happy there?"

"Did you see those women?"

"Yes."

"Then you'll know why I ran away with Malke."

"I don't understand."

"They are all happy living there, waiting to meet their mates and live out the rest of their lives on Pavlovan. None of them want to go to college or explore space, or do anything other than maintain a series of religious traditions that go back for centuries."

"So they do perform a function within your society."

"Yes, I didn't say they were useless, did I? I just said I didn't want to be one of them."

He sat back and crossed one leg over the other. "What kind of religious traditions?"

"They serve the Oracle."

"And you didn't want to do that."

"Not really."

"And were you prevented from doing what you wanted?"

She sighed. "Obviously not, but it still wasn't easy. All that love and concern made me feel worse for wanting to be different than if they'd all hated me and prevented me from leaving."

"I know what you mean. My wife didn't want me to get involved in the super soldier program because she loved me. I chose to ignore her. While I was away being *enhanced* she got sick. I didn't know about it because my superiors told her that taking me out of the program at that point would've killed me. Because she loved me, she chose to die alone."

"That's terrible."

"That's love." He shrugged. "They wouldn't even let me attend her funeral."

"I'm so sorry." She sighed. "And now I feel like an idiot for stamping my foot about being loved too much."

"You shouldn't. That's what I'm trying to say. Sometimes love can be stifling."

"We're going to have to find my mother."

"I got that."

"Chase will help us get organized. Do you think Kaiden will be all right to stay here with the others?"

"I don't see why not."

ON THEIR RETURN to Ash's apartment, Mac made certain to go down to the lower level and visit with his fellow soldiers. He paused in the entrance hall but didn't pick up anything, but contented thoughts and happy people. Everyone seemed to have settled in far more easily than he had expected.

"Mac."

Bevan and Dec were sitting in front of a screen watching

some kind of documentary about Pavlovan. He took a seat on the couch and Dec paused the picture.

"How are things?" Mac asked.

"Pretty good so far. Thanks to Ash, we've had a constant stream of visitors asking us about our current careers, prospects, interests, etc."

"And everyone is okay with that?"

Bevan shrugged. "Why wouldn't we be? Having been thrown out with the trash on Earth, and left to deal with the shit they did to us without any help, being on a planet where telepaths are *valued* is a nice change."

"You're not missing Earth?"

"No." Dec sat forward and focused his intelligent gaze on Mac. "Why—are you?"

"Not at all, but I came here because of Dr. Neeve."

"And we came because we trust you and Commander Kaiden." He shrugged. "None of us left anyone important back on Earth. Since being enhanced and discarded we've all struggled to readjust to society and maintain any kind of relationship with our families."

Mac grimaced. "I know."

"But being here?" Dec smiled. "With all these people thinking along with us? It's fucking amazing."

Bevan nodded. "It is."

"I have to go away for a couple of days, is Kaiden around?" Mac said.

"I think he was out on the deck with Roberts."

"Then I'll go and find him." Mac gave the two men a casual salute. "Good to see you both settling in."

Dec waved as he returned his attention to the screen and Mac went out onto the deck that spanned the entire side of the apartment. Kaiden was still out there playing some kind of ball game with Roberts.

"Mac." Kaiden caught the ball and came over, his rare smile breaking out. "How are you?"

"I'm doing fine. I just wanted to check in on you all."

"As you can see. So far so good. No anxiety issues, no demands to be taken back to Earth and no crying in their sleep. This is a positive thing for these men, Mac. None of them are too stupid to appreciate the opportunity."

"I noticed." Mac stared out over the impressive Pavlovan sky scrape. "I have to go away with Neeve for a few days."

"Do you want me to accompany you?"

"No, I think we'll be fine—unless you want to come. I was hoping you'd stay here and keep an eye on the guys."

Kaiden tossed the ball back to Roberts and moved closer to Mac. "You don't need me as a third?"

He didn't sound upset and Mac wasn't getting anything negative telepathically either. "I think we're good, but thanks for the offer."

"Always willing to oblige a fellow officer."

Mac grinned at him. "Thanks, I'll remember that if you ever need me to fill in as a third for you."

"I don't think Neeve would let you."

"If we're really mated, I suppose not. But that's what this trip is about. To find the Oracle and get her decision."

Kaiden's cool gaze searched his. "And you'll abide by what she says?"

"I promised Neeve I would."

"Good man." Kaiden slapped him on the shoulder hard enough to hurt. "I wish you luck. I'll take care of everything here until you get back."

"Thank you, Commander."

"You're welcome."

Two hours later, Mac was on a private shuttlecraft with an increasingly tense Neeve. As the altitude lowered, he looked out of the window onto acres of bright yellow greenness.

"Looks like a tropical jungle down there."

"It's very similar. There's a temple at *Quoxor*. My mother will be there."

"With the Oracle?"

"Kind of." She nodded and pushed her hair out of her eyes. "I'm not the best of companions when my mother is around, so I'll apologize in advance."

"What's the problem?"

"She wants me to be just like her, to *be* her, and I just can't do it."

"I can't imagine anyone telling you what to do."

"You haven't met my mother."

"Is she a powerful telepath like Ash?"

Neeve shuddered. "Way worse than Ash." The shuttle set down and the pilot started on the precautionary checks. "Let's get our stuff."

He stepped out onto the red soil and inhaled a familiar mixture of humidity, damp soil and rotting vegetation, which reminded him of some of his more hair raising missions in Earth's jungles. Allowing his gaze to move upward he marveled at the huge bell shaped flowers and hanging vines that almost obscured the skyline.

"Come on. It's a bit of a hike."

He grabbed his backpack, hefted it over his shoulder and followed Neeve and the two guides up a path cut into the hillside. Around him strange winged creatures called out and were answered by others and the undergrowth bristled with insect activity. As he walked he breathed deep and tried to relax. Meeting the Oracle and Neeve's mother was going to be interesting...

They kept climbing until even his breathing was ragged and

the air seemed thinner. His shirt was soaked with sweat and so was Neeve's. He paused to take a drink of water and looked down on the valley beneath him.

"How much further is it?"

Neeve was drinking water as well. "Not too far." She pointed upward. "Do you see the white buildings up ahead?"

He saw a glimmer of what looked like pearlescent marble shimmering in the dying rays of the sun above him. "It looks like another palace."

"It's the Temple of *Quoxor*."

"And your mother's there?"

"Yes." She hesitated. "Are you still okay with all this?"

"After coming all this way? The least I can do is say hello before you make me walk back down there."

She reached down and cupped his chin. "Thank you, Mac."

They started moving again and within a few minutes they came to the edge of a flat man made plateau tiled with the gleaming white stone with a massive staircase leading up to the next level. Mac wasn't paying particular attention to the architecture because the area was crowded with half-naked men and women who all seemed to be having a wonderful time.

"What's going on?" He asked Neeve.

"It's the festival of life."

"And what exactly does that entail?"

She raised her eyebrows at him. "What do you think?"

She kept moving and he had to follow her, avoiding the hands that grabbed at his clothing or murmured a sexual invitation for him to slow down, strip off and fuck.

"Mac."

He narrowly avoided having his balls stroked by a female with abundant breasts and mounted the stairs where the crowds thinned out.

"This is the temple, proper. We need to remove our shoes."

"And our clothes?"

"Not quite yet." Neeve took an obvious deep breath and reached for his hand. "Let's do this."

He let her lead him up into the much quieter inner realm of the temple. Huge stone statues guarded the walls and a thousand lights flickered overhead. He smelled incense and was reminded of a Buddhist temple he'd visited on Earth. As they approached the highest and smallest of the structures, a murmur arose and spread like the sighing of a breeze. Those in the temple began to drop to their knees as he and Neeve passed them, opening up a straight pathway to a golden throne where a figure dressed all in white sat presiding over the room.

The scale of her telepathic power made Mac stagger as her gaze turned toward them. Neeve urged him forward. It took all his courage not to balk when she rose to greet them and her psychic energy roared through him exposing all his pathetic secrets and weaknesses.

He didn't need her to tell him to kneel. He did it automatically.

"Oracle."

It took him a moment to notice that Neeve had remained standing. The magnificent masked female inclined her head an inch.

"Daughter. Do you bring me this male?"

"Yes."

Mac was still trying to deal with the ramifications of Neeve's mother *being* the Oracle when Neeve pulled him to his feet.

"He is not of this planet."

"I know that, daughter, but he is acceptable to us."

"Are you quite sure?"

The Oracle smiled. "You are the only female alive who would dare to question the word of the Gods." She turned to Mac and placed a hand on his head. "Ian Fraser McNeill, I designate you First Male to the Oracle's First Daughter."

"But—"

Mac shivered as the Oracle turned to Neeve. "Be at peace, Neeve. I will not be argued with here."

Neeve slowly fell to her knees. "I'm sorry, but, are you quite sure about this? I mean he's human and—"

The Oracle held up her hand. "I have spoken. The Gods have spoken. Do you wish to disgrace me here in my own temple First Daughter?"

"No, but—"

Mac jumped as a wave of power washed over him and Neeve lowered her gaze to the floor.

"All *right.* I accept your decree, but I don't like it." She reached for Mac's hand and they were both shaking. "Thank you."

"You will remain here at the temple until I give you leave to return to the capital."

Neeve nodded and they both retreated slowly down the steps. Mac retained his grip on her hand as she led him through a series of ornate rooms and then through a small door out onto a long furnished balcony.

"Oh, dear Gods, *freking hal.*" she whispered and sank down on one of the chairs. "*Heeze.* I'd forgotten how powerful she was." She looked up at Mac. "Are you okay?"

He sat down beside her and held up his hand, which was still shaking. "Barely. It would've been nice if you'd told me your mother *was* the Oracle. It also explains why you were able to get us all away from Earth."

"I didn't want to tell you. I was too scared."

"That's honest, at least." He flopped down onto his back and stared up at the ornate ceiling where several fans slowly turned. "She's fricking terrifying."

She lay down beside him. "I know. Imagine what it was like being her daughter."

He raised himself up on one elbow to look at her. "Is that why you ran away?"

"Partly. I had three older sisters but they all died and suddenly I was the next in line." She swallowed hard. "It's impossible to protect yourself from her. And Gods I tried. I felt like I had to curl up into a tight ball inside my own head to keep her out, to stop her overwhelming me..." She sighed. "And when I did that, I started to lose myself. That's why I ran away to stop being consumed by her love and her attention. That sounds crazy, I know. But I never imagined I'd be under pressure to take her place as the Oracle one day."

"Can she make you?"

"What do you think?"

It certainly explained why Neeve was so bloody hard to get to know. "Damn. Then why did she just confirm me as your First Male?"

"Because the Oracle can have mates." She hesitated. "In fact, she can have as many as she likes."

Mac stared at her. "You're kidding."

"I never joke about my mother." She reached over to pat his hand. "You will always be number one, though."

"Thanks." He grabbed her elbow and brought her down over him. "Where are we right now?"

"In our suite."

"Is it private?"

"As private as you can get in a temple this size."

He wrapped his hand around the back of her neck, brought his mouth to hers and kissed her until she relaxed and kissed him back. She murmured his name and moved against him rubbing her core against the growing swell of his cock.

"I want you, Princess Neeve."

"Don't call me that."

He smiled at her disgruntled tone. *"Right now, right here."*

She wiggled against him and he slipped a hand between their bodies to rub her clit through her damp panties.

"Now that we're all official..." He slid two fingers inside her

and eased them back and forth until she moved with him. *"And I've met the family and survived your mother."* He pressed his thumb hard against her clit. *"And I'm your First Male..."*

"So what?"

He flipped her onto her back and shoved down his pants. *"I'm going to fuck your fucking princess brains out."*

* * *

MUCH LATER, Neeve disentangled herself from a sleeping Mac and headed to the shower. When she emerged onto the balcony, her mother was sitting in one of the chairs. Neeve glanced back at the bedroom where she'd finally persuaded Mac to move to, and considered the open sliding window.

"He's sleeping, Neeve. He won't hear us unless you start an argument with me."

"But I always start an argument with you." Neeve went over to her mother and knelt in front of her. "Oracle."

"I'm not in the temple now, dear. You can call me Mom."

"I've never called you that, you must be confusing me with one of my other siblings."

Her mother patted the seat beside her. "Oh, do sit down, Neeve, and stop being so prickly. Just call me Gisele if you prefer. It is my given name."

"You'd allow me to be so familiar?"

"Only in private. You are my First Daughter now."

"And I still don't want to succeed you as the Oracle."

Gisele's beautiful mouth turned down at one corner. "I can't force you to make that choice, but I do insist that now you have returned to us you at least consider keeping up with your studies."

"I'll do that if you stop bugging me about it, and you tell all my sisters to stop bugging me, too."

"I'll do my best. But you can understand how they worry."

"Then pick one of them! They'd all kill for the position of First Daughter." Neeve was aware that her voice was rising. Something about her mother always reduced her to a teenager stamping her foot.

"I can't do that, Neeve. You know that." Warmth flowed from her mother's mind enclosing Neeve in a telepathic hug. "Your male is very beautiful."

Neeve glanced over at the bedroom where Mac lay sprawled facedown naked on the bed, one long leg bent at the knee and a hand trailing on the floor.

"I suppose he is."

Gisele smiled. "And I understand he has excellent sexual endurance."

"You've been spying on me on Earth all the time, haven't you?"

"I have kept an eye on you. Your mating is of importance to me and your nation."

"Don't tell Mac that or he'll be running for the hills. He's still trying to get his head around the idea of a permanent threesome."

"As my heir, you can have as many mates as you want."

"I know." Neeve forced a smile. "I think I'll just start with this one, okay?"

Gisele reached for her hand. "I was sorry to hear about Malke's death. It must have been very difficult for you left all alone on that strange closed-minded planet."

"Actually, in some ways it was a relief. I didn't have to guard my thoughts as I grieved as no one could pick them up. I do miss him terribly, though. He was so *kind* to me, so...understanding."

"He would've made a good Second to your new First."

"Does that mean our initial triad will remain incomplete?"

"Oh no, I don't think so. In fact, this evening I've arranged for you and Mac to mingle with the revelers who have come to enjoy the festival of life."

"You think we'll find a third here?" Neeve frowned at her mother. "What do you know that I don't?"

Her mother's silvery laugh chimed like bells. "Oh Neeve, love. I'm the *Oracle*. What *don't* I know?

MAC HELD tight to Neeve's hand as they wandered through the temple. She was attempting to explain what the architecture and art meant to the Pavlovans and he was doing his best to take it all in. People who wanted to congratulate them on their union or simply to bow down at Neeve's feet kept interrupting them. Luckily, she seemed to find it as uncomfortable as he did.

A soft command flowered in Mac's head and he instinctively turned toward the dais where the Oracle sat on her throne, smiling and waving at the crowds. He'd woken up to find the Oracle, or Gisele as she'd asked him to call her in private, sitting with Neeve on the balcony discussing something about potential new duties. It had taken him a moment to realize he was stark naked and that she was happily commenting on the magnificence of his erection before he had the sense to wrap a sheet around his loins and join them.

Neeve squeezed his hand. "She wants us to go up there."

"I got that. Are you okay about all this?"

"The mating with you part is fine, the rest of it? I'm not sure. I never wanted this, Mac. I don't know if I can bear such immense responsibility."

He looked down at her. "Whatever you chose to do, I'll stick it out with you, okay?"

She reached up to kiss his cheek. "That is the nicest thing you've ever said to me. Thank you."

They walked toward the flower-strewn dais and ascended

the steps at the rear. The Oracle stood up and came toward them. She wore a headdress that glittered with colored gems and a white silk robe that concealed very little of her still youthful figure. She stood between them and took their hands in hers leading them toward the edge of the platform.

"My people!"

Her voice rang out over the crowds both physically and telepathically commanding complete attention.

"I give you my First Daughter, Neeve and her First Male Ian McNeill!"

Mac just managed to blink as a shower of flower blossoms were thrown straight at his head The crowd's upturned faces were full of joy as they roared their approval. Mac had the weirdest sensation that he was standing on the edge of a precipice and that his life would never be the same again. Which when he came to think about it, was true. He could never go back to Earth now unless Neeve came with him…

"Are you okay?"

He looked down into her anxious hazel eyes. "Yes, it's just *different*, you know?"

"My mother wants to give you a gift. She asks us to follow her into her chamber."

He followed her through into the private guarded rooms of the Oracle where Gisele awaited them. She snapped her fingers and six males appeared and went down on their knees before Mac.

He looked at the Oracle. "What's this?"

"Your personal guard."

"With all due respect, I'm a super soldier. I can take care of myself."

The Oracle snapped her fingers again, and the men withdrew.

"Neeve's life is still in danger and now that you are her acknowledged mate, so is yours. The Etruscans would like nothing better than to assassinate the Oracle and her newly acknowledged heir. I would ask that while you are with me in the temple that you accept this arrangement."

"You fear for her life here on Pavlovan?"

The Oracle shrugged. "She is the fourth of my daughters to be proclaimed my heir. I doubt all her siblings died naturally. It's the only reason I allowed her to go to Earth for three years."

Neeve put her hands on her hips. "What do you mean, you *let* me? I ran away!"

"Only because I didn't stop you, love." The Oracle smiled and returned her attention to Mac. "I need you to be on your guard."

"Then I will do my best to protect her. I'm still not sure if I need extra help."

"Then you will consider these men your guides for this area and for any trips you intend to make to explore the interior of our country." The Oracle fixed him with a penetrating gaze. "In fact, I have arranged for you to take a trip up the Goachuqu River while Neeve and her siblings spend a few days together."

"You're getting rid of me, already?"

She smiled. "It is necessary."

"But, we've only just been mated."

"Neeve will be fine for the next week. She will need you when you return."

"You know this."

Beside him Neeve stirred, but he didn't take his gaze off Gisele.

"I am the Oracle. I know when a female goes into her breeding cycle."

Neeve sighed and took his hand. "I'll be fine, Mac. You should go and enjoy yourself."

"Are you sure?"

"I have to deal with my sisters at some point. It might as well be now."

"Then I'll do as you wish." He brought her hand to his mouth and kissed her fingers. "When do you want me to leave, Oracle?"

"Tomorrow morning."

He released Neeve and turned to bow to his mate's mother. "You are efficient, I'll give you that."

Her smile was benevolent. "Only because I knew you'd say yes.

11

MAC TESTED THE WEIGHT OF THE PACK HE'D BEEN GIVEN BY ONE of his companions. He still wasn't comfortable using the word, *bodyguard*, but the men around him seemed competent, efficient and well armed. His gaze fastened on one of the males who had a bow and arrow strapped to his back. The man's hair was a fine silver color and was tied at the nape of his neck. His skin was…

The male turned toward him and inclined his head an inch. He wasn't as tall as Mac but was broader in the shoulders.

"Is something wrong with your pack?"

"No, it's fine, I was just…" Mac swallowed. "I noticed you had a bow and arrow rather than a more modern weapon."

The archer came toward him and unhooked his bow in one easy motion. "It is the preferred weapon of my people."

"You're not Pavlovan?"

The man's eyes were silver grey and crinkled at the corners when he smiled. Mac reckoned they were about the same age.

"We're a local tribe called the *Hakron*. We've provided the Oracle and her family with bodyguards for as long as the temple has been here." He handed Mac the bow to examine. "It is an honor to serve the First Daughter's First Male Ian Mac."

"Thank you." Mac lowered his gaze to the beautifully carved shaft of the bow. Something about the male's telepathic aura made him feel like he was swimming in a warm sea, lulled by the pull of a gentle tide... he forced himself to concentrate. "May I know your name?"

"It's Ulluiao."

Mac tried to get his tongue around that and failed miserably. "Yoliow?"

"Not quite." His companion repeated it more slowly.

Mac frowned. "The nearest I can get to it in my language is Willow."

"I do not know that word."

Mac met the man's interested gaze. "It's a tree we have on planet Earth. It tends to thrive best by the riverside because it needs lots of water to survive. Despite its fragile appearance, it is incredibly strong because, unlike most trees on Earth, it has the ability to bend and not break in a storm."

"I like that," Willow mused. "The ability to be strong yet to bend. It is something we all should strive to achieve, is it not?"

Mac found himself nodding in agreement. "The leaves and bark are pale green and the branches hang down to the ground like a curtain."

"Green like my skin? Willow stroked a broad hand over his arm. "Then it is a fitting name, and one I will be proud to bear." He retrieved his bow from Mac's unresisting grasp. "Are you ready to leave now, Ian Mac? We have much we wish to share with you."

He'd already said goodbye to Neeve and left her with about a dozen of her siblings. She looked resigned to her fate rather than annoyed, which had made him feel a lot better about leaving her. Shouldering his pack, he took one last look at the temple complex and followed Willow out through a narrow gate and onto the mountain beyond.

IT TRULY WAS A BEAUTIFUL COUNTRY, as unlike his native Scotland as any place in the universe could be. He paused at the top of a cliff to watch a waterfall pour over into the valley below. Heated steam rose from the pool at the bottom and the roaring of the water was loud enough to prevent him hearing the words Willow mouthed at him. He pointed at his ear and shook his head.

"This is a sacred spot."

Mac almost jumped as Willow's soft voice entered his thoughts telepathically instead.

"It is certainly beautiful."

"The first Oracle came to bathe in the pool below, and the first shrine was built down there to worship her."

"How long ago was that?"

"I am not sure. But my forefathers claim at least fifteen generations of our people have guarded this secret valley and the sacred places within."

"That's a long time." Mac shifted his backpack onto his other arm.

Willow touched his shoulder. *"We will be making camp for the night on the other side of this valley."*

"Good." He winced and stretched his spine. *"I'm out of condition."*

"I am told that it is the altitude that causes fatigue. You will grow used to it in time."

"I hope so."

Mac followed Willow over the narrow bridge that connected the two sides of the gorge, one hand firmly grasping the guide rope. His biometric enhancements would react to the change in his environment eventually, but the long space journey plus the lack of physical activity had definitely slowed him down. His body was racing to catch up with too many changes at once.

Despite his initial misgivings, he was damn grateful to be surrounded by men who knew the terrain so well.

"Ian Mac."

He looked up from his contemplation of the slippery slate floor to see Willow and Ungar another *Hakron* warrior waving at him. Two of the men had already started gathering wood for a fire, and another was unpacking tents and unrolling sleeping pads.

Mac dumped his bag with the others and turned back to Willow. "What can I do to help?"

"You do not need to do anything, Ian Mac. You are our guest."

"I'm not going to sit around on my arse while you're all working. What can I do?"

"Your arse?" Willow asked.

Mac tapped his backside. "This. Now show me how to put up this tent."

Several hours later after sharing stories and Pavlovan beer around the campfire and eating some kind of meat that he hadn't inquired too deeply about, Mac fought the urge to belch. Each of the tents catered for two men and he was lying alongside Willow in a companionable silence. They'd left the flap of the tent open so that Mac could see the purple and pink night sky.

"The food was good, aye?" Willow murmured.

"It was excellent. Where are we headed tomorrow?" Aware of the others sleeping in their tents alongside theirs, Mac tried to keep his voice down.

"We will follow an ancient path through the jungle to a larger lake and hot springs which many claim to have healing properties."

He always forgot that everyone on Pavlovan was telepathic... Sometimes it was damn useful.

"Sounds good."

"Where exactly are you from, Ian Mac?"

"Scotland."

Willow shifted up on one elbow to look down at Mac, his silver hair now falling over his shoulder onto his naked chest. *"It is like Pavlovan?"*

"I've hardly seen enough of Pavlovan to judge. We obviously have some common ancestors and there are other similarities, but overall this place seems warmer and the colors are..." He hesitated trying to think of the correct words and then realized he didn't have to. Opening his mind to Willow, he simply showed him his own memories of Scotland, of his family and where he'd grown up.

"It is a beautiful, stark place." Willow sighed. *"I am surprised you could bring yourself to leave it."*

"It wasn't that hard. Telepaths are rare and were initially only valued by the military and used for their own purposes."

"Used? What do you mean?"

"The government took soldiers like me who showed evidence of basic telepathic talent, and used various methods to enhance us both physically and biologically to produce their version of super soldiers."

Willow squeezed Mac's shoulder hard. *"That is an abomination. I don't even think the Etruscans do that to their telepaths."*

"They just exterminate them, correct?"

"Yes, but to force you to serve their purpose is wrong. I'm no longer surprised you wanted to leave."

"There was another reason." Mac smiled like the besotted idiot he was. *"I met Neeve. If I hadn't been part of that government program I would never have been able to help her."*

"And that would've been a tragedy for our nation."

"Well, I wouldn't call it that, but I don't regret following her here."

"I think you underestimate your importance, First Male." Willow leaned over Mac and dropped a kiss on his forehead. *"Good night. We have an early start in the morning."*

He rolled over onto his side and went quiet leaving Mac staring at the roof of the tent. Was it usual for males to kiss other male's goodnight up here? It had happened so quickly that he hadn't had time to react. He shifted his hand down to cup his balls. Dammit of course he had, he was a fucking super soldier who hadn't felt threatened by Willow's kiss at all.

That was weird.

Mac moved onto his side until he was facing away from Willow and promptly fell asleep.

THE PAVLOVAN EQUIVALENT of the sun shining into the tent woke Mac from a deep sleep. There was no sign of Willow, but the scent of coffee and something fried wafted in, along with the warmth of the day, and encouraged him to get up. When he stepped outside, he saw two of the men sitting beside the fire. One of them was stirring a pot while the other tended to what looked strips of bacon over the flames.

Mac wandered over and exchanged greetings.

"What's that?" He pointed at the thin slices of meat.

"*Kivin.*" Ungar said. "We caught one in a trap last night and we're drying out its flesh to carry with us deeper into the forest where there won't be so much to hunt."

"Makes sense." Mac leaned in to smell the ribbons of meat. "It's like jerky."

"Jer Kee?" Ungar looked puzzled.

"Yes, meat smoked over a fire until it's dry and chewy."

"That sounds like the same thing." Ungar gave Mac a cup of coffee. "Ulluiao said you would appreciate this."

Mac gulped at least two thirds of the brew down in one. "He was right. Where is he by the way?"

"He and Bran are down by the river." Ungar checked the contents of the pot. "You could go and tell them breakfast is ready."

Mac finished off the coffee and refilled his cup. "I'll do that."

It was a beautiful morning, not yet subject to the oppressive humidity and heat that seemed to build up during the day. As he walked along the well-trodden path to the river, he heard the sound of the waterfall and the fainter sound of laughter.

He pushed aside some high grass and came out onto the bank of the river directly above where Willow and Bran had been washing out utensils and other camping stuff and had spread it on the rocks to dry. Now both men were swimming in the crystal clear water and messing around. Mac grinned as Bran suddenly disappeared under the surface only to splutter back up thumping Willow who'd come up underneath him and pulled him down.

In the sunlight, the greenish tinge of Willow's skin seemed to get darker as he smacked the water hard and swam away, Bran in hot pursuit. Reluctant to disturb the men, Mac sat on the bank and waited as they slowly swam back toward him. As they came toward the shore the water level reduced displaying more of Willow's muscular chest, the flare of his hips and the…

"Holy God," Mac whispered. "He's hung like a horse."

Bran ran up behind Willow and wrapped an arm around his waist, his hand slipping down to caress the other male's cock. Willow stopped moving and allowed the touch, his hand coming up to caress Bran's dark hair. After a moment, he gently disengaged Bran's fingers from the rising swell of his cock and shook his head.

Mac realized he'd been holding his breath as Bran laughed and moved away to pick up his clothes and attend to the packing up of the items on the rocks.

Willow angled his head to one side and stared straight up at Mac, who couldn't move. He needed to look away, to break the silence, to…

"Do the males on your planet not kiss each other Ian Mac?"

"Some of them do."

"Does it offend you?"

"Not at all." Mac swallowed hard as Willow came up the bank

toward him, his movements graceful and sure. Water gleamed on his green skin making him look like some kind of Gaelic nymph from Mac's mother's stories of the Fae. It was hard to keep his gaze on Willow's face when his enormous cock was more at his eye level. Mac scrambled to his feet.

"Do you kiss men, Ian Mac?"

"Personally? No, I've never felt the need."

Willow's smile was slow. "That is a pity, I think." He glanced back at Bran. "I must help Bran gather the supplies. Did you want something in particular?"

"To tell you that breakfast is ready."

"Then tell Ungar that we shall be right there."

Mac gestured awkwardly at the rocks. "Do you need any help?"

"No, we can manage." Willow pushed a strand of escaping silver hair behind his ear. "Go back and make sure you eat plenty of food. You will need your energy today."

By the time the Pavlovan sun was overhead, Mac was sweating like a pig and had a headache from the increasingly high altitude. Ungar shouted something and they all came to a halt in the shade of some large trees. Mac sank down to his knees and stayed there until someone thrust a water bottle under his nose.

"Drink this." Willow squatted down beside him, his silver gaze concerned. "You should rest for a while."

"I'm okay. It's just taking my biotech a while to catch up with this new environment."

A bedroll appeared behind him and Willow urged him to sit on it and used both their packs as a back and headrest. For once in his life, Mac didn't argue as he struggled to breathe and adapt.

"Do you need a healer?" Willow asked.

"No, if I rest for a while, I'll be good. Let me contact Kaiden and see if he has any way of monitoring what's going on inside me."

"Kaiden is a telepath?"

"Yes and my commanding officer."

"Your mate, too?"

"No." An image of him and Kaiden in bed with Neeve flooded his senses. Willow's breath hissed out and he rose to his feet.

"I'll speak to the others."

Mac closed his eyes and gathered his energy, aware that he'd been too tired to shield properly and that Willow had probably got an eyeful, or worse, a mindful of Mac's recent sex life that he probably didn't need. But then Willow was a Pavlovan so it was unlikely that he'd be shocked.

"Kaiden?"

"Mac. Where are you? You're very faint."

"My biotech is acting up. Can you do a diagnostic from there?"

"Yes, if you give me the necessary access."

"Go ahead." Mac focused down again, dropped his shields and opened his mind to Kaiden completely. Around the peripheral of his consciousness, he felt Neeve's start of surprise and the quickly blocked reactions of his bodyguards.

"I need more from you." Kaiden said. *"Can you amp it up?"*

Mac jumped as someone touched his shoulder and he opened his eyes to find Willow kneeling beside him again.

"Let me help you. Give me your hand."

He didn't even think about saying no, but accepted Willow's strong-fingered grip and the rush of his telepathic power streaming outward to join with Mac's and project onward to Kaiden.

Damn…it was like a blast of adrenaline, or the finest shot of malt whisky he'd ever tasted.

"*Got it. Who's that with you? It's not Neeve. Did you find your third after all?*" Kaiden sounded amused.

"*It's Willow.*"

He felt Willow's mind separate a little from his and engage with Kaiden's more deeply.

"*A pleasure to meet you, Kaiden. Do not worry about your male. I will keep him safe.*"

Kaiden chuckled. "*Not my male, Willow. Talk to Neeve about that one.*" He paused for a second. "*Mac, your readings are off. You need to allow the biotech time to regenerate properly.*"

"*That's what I thought. There's no other damage, though?*"

"*None that I can see. You're just pushing too hard. Sleep in for a day or two and you should be fine. Your levels are already rising and adapting.*"

"*Good to know, thanks for checking.*"

"*You're welcome. Give my best to Neeve. Over and out.*"

Mac let out his breath and realized he was still holding Willow's hand. "Thanks for your help."

"You are welcome, Ian Mac. I have spoken to my companions. They will move ahead as planned and set up camp at the hot springs further into the valley. You and I will rest here for a while, and then take an easier route to meet up with them this evening."

"Sounds like a plan." Mac's eyes were already closing and he didn't hear Willow stand up or all the others leave.

WILLOW FELT RATHER THAN HEARD IAN MAC WAKE UP behind him.

"Coffee, Ian Mac? I have more water for you, too."

"That would be great."

Willow waited as Ian Mac struggled to sit up against his pack and threw off the blanket placed over him. His black hair was damp with sweat and his clothes stuck to his body.

"God, it's hot."

"Are you hungry?"

"Not really."

"You should still eat." Willow came over and gave Ian Mac the mug of coffee and an energy bar.

"Not dried *kivin?*"

Willow chuckled. "We don't have to do everything the old way. This is a far better way to get nutrients into you fast."

"And it tastes about the same." He ate the bar and sipped the scalding hot coffee.

Around them the jungle slumbered in the simmering heat. When he'd finished Willow handed Ian Mac his water bottle.

"Drink this. When you're done, we'll walk down to the river and replenish our supply."

He rose to his feet, locked his hands and raised them over his head stretching out his limbs. Ian Mac's gaze followed the motions of his body, but when Willow tried to catch his eye, he looked away as if he was embarrassed to be caught staring. It was hard to understand the other male sometimes.

"How long was I out?"

"Not very long. We still have plenty of time to reach camp before it gets dark."

"Good." Ian Mac sighed. "I'm used to being the super soldier, not the one lagging behind."

"There is nothing to be ashamed of. You will soon become accustomed to our world." Willow held out his hand to pull Ian Mac to his feet. "Let's go down to the river."

Ian Mac still wore a black T-shirt that now stuck to his skin, green camouflage pants and thick military boots. He was taller than Willow by half a head but not as wide shouldered. His eyes were a dark blue color that reminded Willow of the Pavlovan night sky.

"Come."

Willow picked up the half-dozen empty water bottles and slung them over his shoulder. He'd already abandoned his coat, his shirt and his footwear. If it stayed this hot, he was contemplating taking off his pants and reverting to his native dress of nothing but a few strategic leather straps for the remainder of the journey. He wondered what Ian Mac would make of that.

They reached the riverbank and Willow set the bottles down and started to unlace his pants.

"What are you doing?"

He glanced back at Ian Mac and hid a smile. "I'm going to wash off in the river after I fill these bottles." He allowed his gaze to sweep over his companion. "If you're hot, you should join me."

An image from Ian Mac's head escaped and Willow saw himself and Bran messing around in the river the previous day. Bran's hand was on Willow's cock.

Interesting that Ian Mac had noticed that... Willow continued to strip, his keen hearing picking up the whisper of laces being untied and the soft hiss of a zipper being lowered. He stepped into the water and waded out into the center of the stream enjoying the coolness against his skin. Keeping his back to the bank, he went deeper until he was able to duck his head under completely.

When he surfaced, Ian Mac was also in the river. His skin was pale and his chest was dusted with black hair that arrowed downward below the surface line. With a groan he sank into the water and disappeared.

"Does that feel better, Ian Mac?"

"Damn right it does."

Willow rolled onto his back and floated on the water, closing his eyes against the insistent glare of the sun. He was aware of Ian Mac floating beside him, but content to enjoy the moment.

"Kaiden isn't my mate."

Willow kept his eyes closed and his body relaxed. *"So he said."*

"I wouldn't wish for you to get the wrong impression."

"About what?"

"About what I might have inadvertently shared with you when I was too tired to shield earlier."

"That you and Kaiden share a bed?"

"There are very few telepaths on Earth. Neeve needed two males to see her through her mating cycle. Kaiden and I were volunteered."

"But you do not consider him your mate even though you fuck him?"

"I haven't fucked him, I've—"

The image Willow received from Ian Mac's mind this time made his cock jerk to attention. He swallowed hard.

"Did you like doing that to him?"

For a long moment Ian Mac didn't communicate and then he sighed. *"Yeah, I did."*

"But you told me you don't kiss males. So you didn't kiss him while you did that? You didn't kiss his cock as well?"

"No. I don't...do that."

"Or let a man do it to you." Willow flipped over onto his stomach and swam away from Ian Mac. It didn't make any difference. He could swim to the other side of the Pavlovan Ocean and he'd still be aware of this male. *"In my society, it is permissible for anyone to touch anyone who welcomes such contact."*

"So I noticed."

"You saw Bran touch me?"

"Yes."

Willow stopped swimming and started to tread water. *"You were offended by that."*

"I...don't know. You have to understand that on Earth, we tend to bond with one other person, that's it. I'm not used to the Pavlovian idea of threesomes or the Hakron idea of casual sex."

"Yet you allowed Neeve, your mate, to sleep with Kaiden."

"That was different. The choice was hers. She needed another male, and Kaiden was available."

"And you shared him, too."

"I did not, I—"

"I saw what you did, Ian Mac." Willow resurfaced right next to the other man and placed his palm flat on his chest. *"And what about me? What if I offered myself to you as Kaiden did? Would you touch me? Would you make me come for you?"*

He slid his hand lower, down over Ian Mac's tight stomach and wrapped his fist around the swell of his thick cock.

"Well?"

Ian Mac groaned and surged forward in Willow's tight grip. "God..."

Willow drew a slow breath and allowed his mind to envelop Ian Mac's. It was like stroking down the raised spines of an *Arkarda*. He didn't do anything except hold his companion's throbbing cock and wait for the frantic beat of his heart to slow down under his palm. The first touch of Ian Mac's mind against his was like the hesitant lick of a man tasting another male for the first time and just as potent.

Willow continued to breathe and simply experience the sense of Ian Mac allowing him inside. A skilled hunter knew that patience was the most important quality needed to lure his prey and he'd waited a long time for this moment.

A very long time.

He could wait awhile longer. Keeping his mind locked with Ian Mac's, he slowly released the other man's cock and pushed gently away from his side.

"Don't..."

Willow shoved his wet hair out of his eyes and smiled. "When you're ready, Ian Mac you know where I am. Now let us continue our journey. If we don't move on soon it will be too dark to travel."

THE SUN WAS SETTING below the canopy of the jungle-like forest and all the light was being sucked out of the sky. Mac glanced over at his silent companion who walked easily, his pack and Mac's on his shoulder. The unbelievable, unwanted connection he'd formed with Willow in the stream continued to stretch between them like a spider's web glistening with possibilities and fraught with danger.

"We'll be there soon."

As if he'd noticed Mac's sudden attention, Willow finally spoke.

"Good." Mac replied.

They walked on, his boots crunching loudly through the

dead leaves while Willow's bare feet made no sound. Mac stopped walking.

"I want to make something clear to you."

"Go ahead, Ian Mac."

"I'm not used to this—being pursued, being hunted."

"And who do you think is hunting you?"

Mac made an exasperated sound. "You know what I mean. I'm already fucking messed up about all this, and you're…"

"I'm not pursuing you, Ian Mac. If I gave you that impression, I can only apologize." Willow held his gaze. There was nothing in his face or his telepathic stream that was in any way hostile or angry or *anything*.

"You're playing games with my head."

"Not at all."

"You touched my fucking *cock*."

"If I offended you, I apologize again. It is natural for me to touch others. You should know that."

"You touch all the men you know like that?"

Willow angled his head on one side and studied Mac. "Why are you so angry? Does the thought of me touching another man offend you, or are you simply jealous?" He turned back to the path and started walking. "I see the lights of the camp. We will be there in a few moments."

Mac stayed where he was and tried to gather the shreds of his temper and his dignity together. What the hell was wrong with him? The Pavlovan nation was doing a fine job of messing with his head. He was a super soldier. A superior being, an athlete, a goddammned killing machine and here he was agonizing over another man like a teenager with his first crush.

His hand clenched into a fist. He was flat-out exhausted that was the problem. A good night of rest should set his biometrics to rights and he'd begin to regain his sense of what was right and what was wrong. That was all it was—a temporary, unnecessary physical glitch.

"What's wrong, Mac?"

"Neeve." He allowed his thoughts to flow out toward her, grateful for the sense of rightness that they were on the same team and that they were meant to be together. *"I miss you."*

"I miss you too. My mother is driving me nuts. I've tried to keep out of your head, but how's the trip?"

"It's fascinating. I'm learning a lot about your history."

"It's a great experience. My mother made us all take the same route when we were kids."

"Did you have Hakron bodyguards, too?"

"Yes. They are amazingly good in that terrain." She hesitated. *"Are you feeling okay? I noticed you needed a boost to communicate with Kaiden earlier?"*

"It's taking a bit of time for my body to adjust to these new conditions, but Kaiden says I should be fine in the next two days."

"Good, because when you come back I'm going to need you."

"I'll be ready for anything by then. I promise you." He found himself smiling as he registered the desire in her voice. Only a few months ago that might have scared him, but now he was raring to go and desperate to get back and claim her again.

"Then I'll be as patient as I can." She paused. *"My Mother says to give her love to Willow, whoever that might be."*

Mac hoped his jerk of surprise didn't register. *"He's one of my bodyguards. I'll pass the message on."*

"Thanks, and I'll let you go."

Mac started walking again, his gaze fixed on the flickering light of the fire ahead, and the shadows of his bodyguards. What did the Oracle want with Willow? Did she already know what had happened in the stream earlier that day? Dammit, of course she did. She was the Oracle. He straightened his shoulders and kept going. A hot meal and a good night's sleep had better straighten him out, or something was going to give…

LATER THAT NIGHT, Mac woke up and realized he was dreaming about Neeve and Willow and that his hand was wrapped around his hard cock. The need to come had forced him out of sleep and into pained, throbbing awareness. Beside him Bran snored away oblivious to Mac's discomfort, which was just as well, because from what he'd seen of his bodyguards, lending another man a hand with an erection was completely acceptable behavior.

He'd intended to avoid Willow over dinner, but he hadn't been given the opportunity. The other man had spent most of his time checking through the supplies, fixing his equipment and had then gone out hunting with Ungar and hadn't returned before Mac had decided to go to bed.

Realizing his chances of getting back to sleep were decreasing with every second, Mac got up and crawled out of the open tent. The two Pavlovan moons were bright silver disks of light in the dark purple sky and illuminated the forest without him needing another light source.

Willow and Ungar sat at the fire, cutting and scraping away at some dead animal. Even as Mac watched they finished whatever they were doing, and Ungar rose to his feet, slapped Willow on the shoulder and disappeared in the direction of the stream with the remains of the creature. Mac tensed as Willow cleaned his knife and put it away.

With a sigh, Willow stood up and stretched. Apart from some leather strapping around his groin, he was completely naked and smeared with the dried blood of his kill. Without a backward glance, he turned toward the rocks that bordered one side of their camp and headed toward them.

Mac watched him go and looked back toward his tent where Bran snored on. After seeing Willow he wouldn't be sleeping again. Fueled with a mixture of rage and frustration, Mac went after him. As he found his way between the rocks, he began to smell sulphur and steam, but it didn't deter him.

The path narrowed to a passageway hardly wider than his shoulders with sheer rocks on either side that at some points closed over his head. The smell of minerals grew stronger as did the clouds of moisture billowing from the opening of a cave.

He paused before he went inside. Not because he was unsure of where Willow had gone—he knew that in his soul—but because he still wasn't sure what he was doing, or why he needed to confront a man who had made it very clear that he was interested in Mac in every way possible.

Dammit, he had to sort this out before he went back to Neeve.

With that thought, he went into the cave and almost slipped on the slick uneven surface. He grabbed onto the nearest solid object and stared around the amazing space. Black rocks glinted with a thousand tiny splinters of light mimicking the starry night sky outside and surrounded a series of pools from which rose clouds of steam.

"Hot springs."

His voice echoed around the closed in space. He remembered Willow had mentioned them earlier. A splash drew his attention deeper into the caves. Taking off his shoes, he moved on past the first two pools filled with turquoise water and headed inward.

Willow sat on the edge of one of the pools splashing water over his muscled torso. He made no sign that he knew Mac was there, but he didn't need to. Since that moment in the lake, they were fully aware of each other without even trying. With a soft groan, Willow slid into the pool and ducked his head under the water. When he came back up to the surface he was facing Mac, his expression serene.

"Are you coming in? The water is hot."

Wordlessly, Mac stripped off his T-shirt and pants and got into the pool, hissing at the heat of the water despite Willow's warning. It felt good against his skin and he sunk to the bottom pushing off with his feet to resurface.

Willow sat on the side of the pool, his arms spread wide, his eyes closed, droplets of water slid down his face and over the pale green skin of his hairless chest.

"Sit. There's a ledge here."

Mac swam over and hoisted himself up to sit on the rock. "Listen, Willow—"

The other man turned and put his finger on Mac's lips, his silver gaze calm. "Not now, Ian Mac. I'm tired and I wish to enjoy this sacred place."

"But—"

"Please."

Mac jerked his head away from Willow's touch and fixed his gaze on the other side of the rock pool. He took several long deep breaths aware of Willow enfolding his mind in a blanket of peacefulness that somehow made him feel even more irritated.

"Ian Mac, relax. Stop fighting me."

Mac set his jaw and attempted to block Willow from his thoughts.

His companion gave a quiet chuckle. *"It's too late for that."*

"Get out of my head." Mac clambered out of the pool and stared down at Willow who raised an eyebrow.

"What is it you want, Ian Mac?" Willow got out and came to stand by Mac, water ran down his body in shining rivulets of silver

"You to leave me the fuck alone."

"You are the one who followed me in here. I did nothing to hunt you down or lure you to me."

Mac poked Willow in the chest. "Your very existence is a threat."

"A threat to what?"

Mac shoved Willow hard, but he only rocked on his feet and stayed far too close.

"You don't really want to fight me, Ian Mac."

"You're wrong about that." He drew back his hand, but Willow caught his wrist. "I'm a super soldier. I can rip you apart with my bare hands."

Willow released him. "Then go ahead. But I know what's in your mind. I know the truth and so do you. You just have to allow yourself to believe it." He reached out and cupped Mac's chin. "You don't want to fight me, you want to fuck me and that scares you."

"I do not—"

Willow went down on his knees and nuzzled the growing swell of Mac's shaft through the clinging fabric of his wet boxers. With a stifled sound, Mac reached down and grabbed Willow's long hair to pull him away and then found himself groaning as Willow sucked the head of his shaft, cotton and all into his mouth.

"Let me do this for you, Ian Mac."

And God help him, now he wasn't shoving Willow away, he was shoving himself deeper into his mouth, one hand clutched in his hair, the other pushing down his boxers to give the man more access to his throbbing, needy cock. And Willow didn't disappoint him, swallowing him whole and sucking every inch of him deep.

Mac closed his eyes as a rising tide of lust, need and *fear* swept over him.

"It's all right, Ian Mac, I have you safe. Let me do this for you, let me make you come."

He let himself fall into the complexities of Willow's mind, the shadows, the need to please him, the exquisite enjoyment his companion took in pleasuring him. As he sucked Mac's cock, Willow also cupped his balls, his thumb sliding up and down the soft skin of his taint to rub and circle Mac's puckered hole.

"God—" Mac started to come in endless thick waves his hips jerking forward to cram as much of himself down Willow's throat as he could. He rocked back on his heels only his grip on Willow's head stopping him from falling to the ground. With great care he peeled each finger from Willow's hair and sat down on the nearest flat rock with a thump.

Willow stayed on his knees facing Mac and looked down at his own throbbing cock. He was already wet. With one finger he circled the slit of his crown drawing even more moisture out, and used it to slick his fingers down over his hard shaft. Still maintaining their telepathic link, he started to play with his cock and balls, rubbing and squeezing, sharing each internal shudder of pleasure and hint of his desperate need to come, making Mac shiver in his turn.

Licking his middle finger, Willow eased it lower until he could reach past his taint and circle his hole, easing the tip deeper with every undulation.

"Do you like this, Ian Mac? Seeing my fuck myself? Shall I push my finger all the way in, add another, add more?"

Mac wasn't aware of moving but the next second he was kneeling in front of Willow, his gaze fixed on the motions of his hands. Every time Willow pushed his finger deep he trembled with the sensation and shared it with Mac whose own cock filled out again in helpless response.

"I...want..."

"What do you want, Ian Mac?"

He licked his lips. *"I want my fingers in you."*

Willow shuddered. *"Yes."*

Mac crawled around behind him and smoothed one shaking hand over Willow's arse before running his finger down between his buttocks. Slicking up pre-cum on his fingers, Mac eased one deep inside Willow, enjoying the burst of pleasure that flowered through their locked minds.

With a guttural sound, Willow reached back between his legs and grabbed Mac's cock and started to rub it in time to Mac's finger thrusts. Mac reciprocated by wrapping his body around Willow's and finding his cock.

Pleasure blossomed and then was overtaken by the sheer, driving need to come as Mac forgot caution and focused on giving Willow every ounce of pleasure he could wring out of him. They came together, minds melding into a red-hot flare of passion, which left Mac gasping and coming hard.

WITH A GROAN, Willow rolled over, taking himself and Ian Mac back into the hot water pool, their limbs still tangled, their hearts racing. Willow slicked his hair out of his face and smiled at Mac.

"Better than fighting, aye?"

Ian Mac grabbed his shoulder and held him slightly away from him. "I shouldn't have done that."

"Touched me?" Willow shrugged. "I wanted you to."

"And I still shouldn't have done it. I'm mated to Neeve."

"So?"

"That means something to me."

"As it should, First Male. I don't understand why you are upset."

"Because I shouldn't have touched you while I'm in another relationship."

Willow frowned. "She will not mind."

"She might not, but I will. I was fucking disloyal to both of you." Ian Mac backed away and climbed out of the water. "I'm sorry, Willow. I promise I'll stop bugging you and keep away for the rest of this trip."

"But—"

Ian Mac turned away, picked up his clothing and walked out.

Willow stayed where he was and tried to understand what the *heeze* was going on. Was Ian Mac blind? Did he really think

Neeve would object to their joining? She was a Pavlovan and the Oracle's chosen heir. For a wild moment, he considered chasing after the other male and showing him just how hard it was going to be to walk away.

But that would achieve nothing. Willow let out a long slow breath. His heart ached, and for the first time in many years he questioned the certainties he had lived his life by. Was it possible that his interpretation of the Oracle's prophecy was wrong?

A wave of sadness flooded over him. He would mediate and pray on the matter as they headed back to the temple. He would also do as he'd been asked, and keep away from Ian Mac.

13

"They are back, daughter."

Neeve grinned at her mother and put down the scroll she'd been studying. "That's great and just in time, too. If it's okay with you, I'll go down and meet Mac at the first gate."

"I'd rather you waited until he reached the secured compound."

Neeve rose. "Sure."

Her mother gave her the Oracle's benign smile. "Thank you for not arguing with me, First Daughter."

"I'm trying not to, Gisele." Neeve came around and kissed her mother's cheek. "I'm glad you noticed."

"May I make a suggestion, Neeve?"

Neeve paused. "It depends on what it is."

"Don't rush to make judgments. Listen carefully to all the evidence and make your decision based on the truth of the situation, rather than how it first appears."

"What's that? The Oracle quote for the day?"

"Just something to think about."

Neeve waved and headed out of the library. Since reuniting with her mother and sisters she'd found herself becoming more

163

forgiving of their ways and far more understanding of the burden her mother was under to provide spiritual guidance for an entire nation who worshipped her as a god. Three years away from Pavlovan had helped her appreciate the stability of her planet. She still didn't want to take the job, but at least she had mended matters with her family.

If she could only convince her mother to allow her far more suitable sister Reyna to become the next Oracle, her life would be awesome. Keeping her shields high so that she could surprise Mac, she walked down the seven levels to the much less public secure entrance to the temple's private apartments.

The low hum of voices caught her attention and she slowed on the curve of the spiral staircase. Was that Mac? Who was he conversing with so urgently? A wave of tangled emotions shot through her mind and she instinctively raised her shields even higher.

It *was* Mac, but whom was he talking to?

She peeked around the corner and caught a flash of long fair hair and then a hand wrapped around the person's neck pulling them back out of sight. Hardly daring to breathe, Neeve crept closer, but there was nothing more to hear only the sense of complex emotions flying through the air, of defeat, of despair, of *longing*…

Mac came around the corner, his expression distraught and pulled up short at the sight of her.

"Neeve!"

She stayed where she was, arms folded over her chest.

He started toward her. "I didn't expect to see you."

"So I gathered. Who was that?"

His shields slammed down. "Who was what?"

"That person you were talking to?"

He shoved a hand through his damp hair. "I can't tell you."

"You're my *mate*."

"And I owe you an apology." He hesitated. "Can we talk about this somewhere else?"

She turned on her heel and went back up the stairs until she reached their suite of rooms. Leaving the door open for him, she went inside and stationed herself in the middle of the floor. Mac came in, shut the door behind him and dropped his backpack on the floor.

"Spill." Neeve snapped.

He straightened and looked her in the eye. "As I said, I owe you an apology. I forgot that I was on a different planet and that the cultural expectations here aren't the same as on Earth. I inadvertently created a situation where I hurt another Pavlovan."

"What the *heeze* does that mean? Did you sleep with another female?"

He blinked at her. "No, of course not."

She finally remembered how to breathe. "Good. So what did you do?"

He rubbed a hand over the back of his neck. "Nothing that will ever happen again. I know this is asking a lot of you, Neeve, but could we leave it at that?" He lowered his shields and opened his mind to her. "I'm the one to blame for everything. The other Pavlovan didn't do anything that wasn't perfectly acceptable in your culture."

Her hands curled into fists. Gods, she was *jealous*...Were Pavlovans able to feel that way? Perhaps only about their mates.

Remembering her mother's advice to breathe deeply and consider before she became all judgey, she thought about what *she'd* asked Mac to accept about her planet, and how hard he'd tried to adapt for her sake. She'd made it a condition of their mating that he consent to be in a threesome maybe even with another male. Could *she* accept that his decision to stay with her had led him into an encounter with a Pavlovan who wouldn't have understood that Mac wasn't used to their ways?

"Was this Pavlovan mated?" She hated herself, but she had to ask.

"I don't know." He frowned. "How would I know that?"

"Did you sense any other connections?"

"No."

"Did you have to tell this Pavlovan about me, or were they aware that I existed?"

"They knew you existed."

"Then they were probably not mated to another." She let out her breath. "I don't like it, Mac. I know that after all my preaching to you I shouldn't care, but I don't like the thought of you sharing anything with anyone but me."

He almost cracked a smile. "You sound just like I used to before I met you." He came toward her, his hand outstretched. "Will you forgive me? I fucked up, I regret hurting you more than I can say."

She let him gather her into his arms and laid her cheek against his chest. He smelled of the outside with a hint of the minerals from the springs. She inhaled again and wrapped one arm around his neck.

"Take me to bed."

He placed his fingers under her chin and made her look at him. "You're okay about this? I swear, I'll tell you—"

She blocked his words with her mouth and with a groan; he picked her up in his arms and took her into the bedroom.

SEVERAL HOURS LATER, she woke up and leaving Mac to sleep, she dressed in a silk robe and headed out onto the balcony. She almost screeched when a green shadow detached itself from the foliage beside the security wall and bowed.

"First Daughter. I didn't mean to startle you. The Oracle ordered us to secure your suite."

She placed a hand over her rapidly beating heart and nodded. "It's okay. You're one of the *Hakron*, aren't you?"

"Yes, First Daughter. My name is Ungar. I am honored to be one of your First Male's bodyguards."

He had long brown hair with three small braids on each side of his face and warm hazel eyes.

"It's good to meet you, Ungar."

"We will be patrolling the balcony area every night while you and the Oracle are in residence. Ulluiao is stationed by the Oracle's suite."

"Did you say Willow?"

He paused. "Your First Male could not pronounce the name properly and that's what he chose to call him. Ulluiao is the head of our unit. Do you know him?"

"My mother mentioned him. How did the trip go?"

"Ian Mac found it hard to keep up at first, but he proved a worthy companion. He was not too proud to share the workload even though he was exhausted."

"That sounds just like him." Neeve strolled further away from the windows and Ungar followed. "Did you stop in any of the villages?"

"Only to get supplies on the way back. We had to stay an extra day at the hot springs so that your mate could complete his 'biotech' repairs." Ungar smiled. "On the return journey we met up with two parties traveling to worship at the temple. Word has spread of your joining. They were all eager to meet your First Male."

Neeve nodded. So the person that Mac had been talking to at the security gate had either come back with him, or had been in the temple all along. Not that she cared. She was beyond that now. Perhaps it was one of the temple visitors who would be leaving fairly soon, and had merely thought to celebrate their pilgrimage with some sexual excess by propositioning the Oracle's daughter's male.

Her male...

But Mac had placed the blame squarely on himself. She let out a breath and studied the calmness of the night sky. This jealousy thing wasn't pretty. She felt like a hypocrite. She had to let go of what had happened, give Mac the benefit of the doubt and move on. He deserved her trust.

"Did my First Male make particular friends with any of the females you met?"

Ungar's smile was slow to come and full of quiet humor. "No, First Daughter, he did not. He spoke only of his love and regard for you."

"Good." Neeve smiled back at the bodyguard. "Thank you."

He hesitated. "If you wish to learn more about how the journey, you should speak to Ulluiao. He and your First Male spent much time together."

"I'll do that. Thanks Ungar."

"You are most welcome. Good night, First Daughter."

He bowed and faded back into the shadows and Neeve hesitated. Ungar had said Willow was just along the balcony. She wasn't ready to go back to sleep yet, so she might as well go and make his acquaintance.

She turned to her right and walked along the side of the private quarters and around the corner to where her mother had her suite.

"First Daughter."

She nodded at the blond-haired man who guarded her mother's door. He exuded a sense of calm resolution that she envied and something deeper, something he instantly concealed behind the intricacies of his complex telepathic shields.

"You are Willow?"

He bowed. "Yes, First Daughter."

"May I speak to you for a moment?"

"Of course. How may I help you?"

She took the seat he held out for her. "I was wondering how your trip with my First Male went."

His fingers tightened around the shaft of his spear. "Did he speak of me?"

"No, not at all."

"Ah."

"It's just that Ungar said you spent the most time with Mac, and I wondered if he seemed okay."

He frowned. "I am not familiar with that last word, First Daughter. What does it mean?"

"Okay? It means all right. I must have picked it up on Earth. I meant was Mac behaving normally?"

"Apart from being fatigued, I would imagine he was behaving perfectly normally for a human."

"Did he offend you?"

His smile seemed forced. "Not at all, First Daughter. He is an honorable, man who will remain loyal to you."

She glanced down at her hands. "He didn't seem interested in any other females, did he?"

"No, First Daughter." His voice was gentle. "Why would you even think that?"

"Because I'm an idiot?" She rose to her feet before she started bawling. "Thanks. It was nice to meet you."

He went as if to touch her and then drew back his hand. "The pleasure was all mine. I have longed for this moment for my entire life."

She stared into his eyes and couldn't look away. "Willow..."

He was the first to break contact. "You do not need to worry about anything, First Daughter. Ian Mac will never give you cause to doubt him, I swear it on the Gods of Pavlovan."

"You have the sight?"

His smile was wry. "In this case, I think you might say that I have. Good night, First Daughter."

"Good night, Willow."

Neeve retraced her steps and returned to bed. She wasn't proud of herself for snooping, but at least she felt a little better about what might have occurred. As she climbed into bed, Mac reached for her and enfolded her in his arms.

Of course, if she really wanted to know the truth, all she had to do was ask the Oracle...

Neeve buried her face against Mac's chest. That was not going to happen. She also had a sensation that if her mother had wanted her to know about what went on, she would've already told her. So it couldn't be bad...could it?

MAC WOKE up with a headache and found Neeve had already gone. His sleep had been troubled by dreams of Willow walking away again. What the hell was wrong with him? Even as his bodyguards had said their goodbyes and dispersed at the gate the day before, he'd grabbed hold of Willow and hugged him hard, aware of the light kiss dropped on his head and the gentle words of forgiveness and regret flowing from his companion.

And then Neeve had come around the corner and stopped him doing something stupid like chasing after Willow and begging him not to leave him...

So much for his ice-cool status as a killing machine. He was a fucking emotional wreck who should never have been allowed off Earth.

"Come down to breakfast when you are ready, First Male."

The Oracle's sweet but demanding voice came into his head and he leapt out of bed as if she was standing over him. He intended to politely ask Neeve's mother when it would be convenient for them to return to the capital city, citing concern for his men as his reason for their departure. But that wouldn't be for at least three days. Neeve was due to go into her mating cycle.

He took a very fast shower, dressed in his favorite uniform of a black T-shirt and military issue khaki pants and made his way down the stairs to the kitchen. To his surprise, the Oracle, or as she'd asked him to call her, Gisele, sat alone at the table drinking some kind of juice and nibbling at chunks of tropical fruit.

"Ah, Ian, come in and have something to eat."

He took the chair opposite hers and was immediately surrounded by servers who set his usual breakfast of juice, coffee, fruit and odd-shaped doughnuts in front of him. There was also a Pavlovan version of bacon and eggs, but he couldn't get over the sight of blue yolks and green fat to try it. The servers disappeared as quickly as they had arrived.

"Where's Neeve?"

The Oracle finished her juice. "She's in my study trying to complete the task I allotted her before she goes into her mating cycle."

"Then I suppose I should expect to meet up with her in our suite."

"Yes, I should imagine so." Gisele wiped her mouth with her napkin. "I will select a third for you."

Mac lowered his fork. "Is that necessary?"

"It is not a reflection on you or your stamina, Ian. You will need help if you are to keep the First Daughter satisfied."

"If you insist."

"I do. My daughter's happiness is very important to me." She paused. "Which is why I was concerned when she seemed a little distraught this morning.

"Distraught?"

Gisele fixed him with her direct blue gaze. "Yes. She thinks you cheated on her with a Pavlovan female."

"I've already told her that I didn't, and, with all due respect, I'm not sure why she involved you in this matter."

"She wanted me to tell her the truth. I can, you know." She paused. "But I'd much rather she heard it from you."

"I didn't fuck anyone."

"You penetrated Willow with your fingers and worked his cock until he came. Does that not count because he is a man?"

"Of course it counts." Mac exhaled. "I've already apologized for that, too."

"To whom?"

"To both of them."

"As the mother of your mate *and* the Oracle, might I suggest that you tell Neeve the truth?"

"She accepted my apology. She said everything was fine."

"Which is why she asked me to tell her exactly what had happened. She might think that she has no right to chastise you because Pavlovan society wouldn't, but inside, she is unhappy and such things can ruin even a telepathic relationship." She paused. "I'm sure you don't want that to happen."

"No, Oracle." Mac said as politely as he could.

"Good." Gisele smiled. "Now, finish your breakfast. You will need all your strength to serve my daughter."

NEEVE PACED the balcony of her and Mac's suite, and wondered where the hell he was. Someone was blocking his thoughts from her, and the only person powerful enough to do that to a mated couple was her mother.

That could never be good. It made her scared, and she hated being scared.

A tap on the door made her go back inside and fling open the door.

"Mac, where the *heeze* have you—"

"First Daughter." A Hakron male with long fair hair and light green skin bowed low to her. "I am Ulluiao. We met last night. The Oracle sent me to aid your First Male."

"Willow?"

His smile was sweet. "Yes."

"Come in."

She opened the door wide and stepped back, her gaze fixed on his face. He exuded such a sense of calm that she almost felt dizzy. Without thinking, she pushed the door shut and stroked a hand down over his cheek. His mouth quirked up at the corner, and she paused to circle the dimple it revealed. With a sigh, he dropped the barriers that had prevented her seeing into his mind the previous night.

"Do you wish me to undress, First Daughter?"

Blushing she snatched her hand back. "Not yet, Willow. We'd better wait for Mac to arrive. I'm not sure if he's going to go for this."

His fingers closed over hers, and he brought them to his lips and kissed them. Lust roared through her and her knees almost buckled.

"Who the *heeze* are you?" she whispered.

"I am yours." He sank down onto his knees and bowed his head. "You know this."

She found herself nodding as his mind reached out to hers again and they blended seamlessly together. This could not be happening so fast, this could not be happening at *all*. Mac was going to…

Neeve shivered as he pressed his mouth to her mound and inhaled. "You're wet for me First Daughter."

Her fingers crept into his hair and held him still. He didn't try and do anything, but stayed there, his mouth pressed to her mound, the rise and fall of his breathing as calm as his thoughts.

"Mother, if you have Mac there send him back immediately!"

Her mother's laughter echoed in her head. *"You like Willow, don't you?"*

"Like him? I want to strip him naked and eat him up."

"Then do so."

"I can't. Mac won't—"

"Let Mac make that decision for himself. He's already on his way back to you."

Neeve released the block on her mind and the essence of Willow, of everything he was, and everything he might mean to her swamped her anew. This was the kind of meeting of minds that she and her sisters had giggled about in Pavlovan romances. This was freking *unbelievable.* There was nowhere to hide herself from him, no chance of him not finding her. *Gods…*He rubbed his mouth against the thin cotton of her long t-shirt, unerringly finding the edge of her panties beneath and ran his teeth along the top.

This time her knees really did buckle. She caught his shoulder and held on.

"Neeve?"

She looked up as Mac came through the door and went still. His gaze falling to the man who knelt in front of her.

"Willow?" He croaked.

"Yes, Ian Mac. The Oracle sent me."

Neeve waited as Mac walked over and stood beside her, one arm around her waist. His gaze dropped to the hard points of her nipples sticking out from her t-shirt and he inhaled the scent of her arousal that perfumed the air.

"Do you want him, Neeve?"

"Yes. Do you mind?"

Mac shook his head. *"How could I?"*

"Because I'm being such a hypocrite, berating you for touching someone and ten seconds later willing to leap into bed with a second man."

"But this is Willow."

"Yes, it is. Does that make it better for you? That you know him? Can you work with me on this just for the next three days?"

He bent to kiss her throat. "*Yes.*"

She realized she might be babbling, but couldn't seem to stop as the essence of the two males surrounded her sending her hormones wild. "*We can worry about the rest of it later, okay?*"

He bit her neck. "*Yes. Stop worrying.*" He slid his hand higher to cup her breast and then pinch her nipple. "*Let's take this off you.*"

She held her arms up as he pulled her t-shirt over her head, leaving her in just her panties. Still on his knees in front of her, Willow made an appreciative sound and leaned in to nuzzle her.

"*May I have your permission to pleasure her, First Male?*"

Neeve held her breath as Mac looked down at Willow and then sighed. "*Go ahead. I...want to see you with her.*"

"*I wish to serve you both, First Male.*"

Neeve gasped as Willow gently sucked her clit through her cotton panties until it was throbbing in time to her ragged heartbeat.

"*Take them off her.*" Mac said.

Willow slid her panties down her legs and she stepped out of them, her bare ass now pressed against the hard ridge of Mac's cock as he stood behind her watching over her shoulder.

"*Ah, First Daughter, you are beautiful.*" Willow's reverent voice echoed inside her head.

"*Use your mouth on her, make her come.*"

"*It will be my pleasure.*"

The first lick of Willow's tongue against her bare flesh made her whimper with need and Mac groan. She tried to widen her stance, leaning back against Mac until Willow took her right foot and placed it carefully on his left shoulder opening her sex to him. He dipped his head and licked her lavishly like an ice cream, his mouth lingering on her clit, his teeth tugging at her already swollen pussy lips.

She didn't need to tell him what she liked, or what she loved, with the connection so strong between them, he just *knew...*

Mac's hands closed around her breasts, his fingers and thumbs tightening and twisting her nipples in time to Willow's sucking. The intense pleasure overwhelmed her and she climaxed gripping Mac's upper arm and Willow's hair and hanging on for dear life.

"*Bed.*" Mac commanded.

He picked her up and walked through to their bedroom, Willow behind him. After placing her on top of the sheets, Mac stripped out of his clothes and climbed up next to her. Willow waited, his hands at his sides, his gaze switching between her and Mac.

Neeve patted the space on the other side of her. "Come here."

"Yes, First Daughter." Willow hesitated. "Do you wish me to disrobe?"

"God, yes." Neeve breathed. "If that's okay with you, Mac."

Willow smiled. "Ian Mac has seen me naked before. We swam together at the hot springs."

He started to remove his loose white shirt and pants and Neeve forgot to breathe as his superbly fit body emerged. He ran a hand over his already thick shaft spreading the gathering pre-cum. She wanted that cock, wanted it in her fast.

Reaching forward, she caught his shaft in her hand and drew him as near to the side of the bed as she could manage. As soon as he was standing close enough, she leaned over and started to suck him into her mouth. Behind her, Mac groaned as she gradually took more and more, fighting her impulse to gag at Willow's impressive thickness and length.

As she sucked, she shared the sensation with both men. Mac came up behind her and shoved his cock deep in her cunt and held her down over him with one hand wrapped around her hips. The throb of his cock inside her mimicked the pulse of Willow's far down her throat. She tried to move on Mac, but he wouldn't allow it, filling her as completely as Willow was.

It was only when she started to slide her mouth up and down Willow's shaft that Mac allowed her to do the same to his cock. The two men worked together helping her slide between their lengths, their bodies protecting and restraining her as she grew more adventurous.

With a groan, Mac started to pump into her, pushing her onto Willow's cock until all she could do was just take him down her throat and suck as hard as she could. Mac's come shot inside her and Willow came too, his hand still gentle in her hair despite the fierceness of his climax and the intensity of his pleasure.

For a long moment, they all stayed in place and then both men eased themselves free of her and Willow climbed up onto the bed and collapsed next to her.

"That was…wonderful, First Daughter."

She reached out a languid hand and patted his head. "Please call me Neeve."

"If you permit, First Male."

"It's not up to me. Neeve's in charge here. And call me Mac or Ian Mac."

Willow sat up and looked at them both. His hair had come loose from its braid and hung over his shoulder "This is our first time together. I wished to enjoy the formality of the joining."

Neeve grinned at him. "That was formal? I'd hate to see us when we get wild." She shivered as both men responded to her words and both cocks stirred. With them both so focused on her pleasure, Mac might find it easier than he'd expected to accept a stranger in their bed. He'd managed it with Kaiden, but then she hadn't reacted to Kaiden in quite the same way. Had he sensed that yet? She doubted she'd be able to hide anything from him soon.

"May I?"

Mac crawled between her legs and pushed her knees wide apart. He pressed both thumbs to her clit and then slid them through her wetness inside, spreading her wide and making her buck against his hand. Willow moved to her side and sucked and played with her nipples until she started to come again, thrashing against the sheets as Mac added more fingers to his plunging, curling thumbs.

"I want..." She just managed to gasp out the words.

Mac smiled at Neeve, all too aware of her desires and the extraordinary presence of Willow at his side. "You want more cock?" He glanced over at Willow and licked his lips. "She's ready for you."

Willow raised his silver gaze to Mac's. "And I want her, which is how it should be, aye?"

Mac nodded and moved out of the way so that Willow could take his place between Neeve's thighs. He realized he was holding his breath as Willow slowly eased forward into Neeve, his buttocks flexing as he rocked back and forth and gradually impaled her on his impressively thick cock.

He felt them both in his mind, Willow's careful thrusts and Neeve's gasps as he kept filling her and widening her until she was stuffed full of cock and then he kept pressing deeper.

Willow paused, breathing hard. Mac could still see at least two inches of Willow's cock still unsheathed. *"I don't want to hurt you."*

"You won't. I want all of you. Please."

Neeve tilted her hips and took another inch and started to come allowing Willow to finally fit himself fully inside her. Mac imagined he was being filled like that. Could a man take another man that deep and hard? Would he want to?

"I'd fit, Ian Mac, do not worry. I'd have you begging for me to fill you." Willow's lust-filled voice echoed through Mac's head and his cock jerked.

Willow drew back and started to undulate his hips, his cock pistoning in and out of Neeve in long slow strokes that made her whimper and climax again and again. Mac could only watch helplessly as Willow shared the experience with him He gripped his own cock. Neeve flung out her hand and grabbed his shaft too, clutching him almost to the point of pain, and working him in time to Willow's thrusts.

"*Gods...*" Willow shoved deep one last time, and came, his back arched and his whole body shaking with the effort, his hand braced on the bed to stop himself from falling forward onto Neeve. He eased himself free and rolled onto his back his chest rising and falling with each labored breath. Mac lay on Neeve's other side, one hand cupping her mound the other across her waist as she relaxed between them. His fingers grazed Willow's hip and he left his hand there, strangely connected to them both.

If he tried to work out what was going on, he might spoil this miraculous moment of having Neeve and Willow in bed with him. It was like having all his fantasies in one place. If three days were all he would have with them both, he'd take it.

After a while, Neeve's hand closed around his cock and started to rub him. Looking over her body he realized she was doing the same thing to Willow. Careful not to dislodge her working hand, he knelt up and leaned down toward her sex. Willow did the same and he was able to watch Neeve's hand on the other man before they both dipped their heads and set about licking and sucking Neeve to a climax.

His tongue swept over Neeve's already swollen clit and he tasted all three of them, which made him even harder. Willow murmured something and then his tongue tangled with Mac's as they both penetrated her cunt.

"*Wait.*" Neeve said.

Mac froze, thinking for a second she was going to call him

out for touching Willow, but she was struggling to sit up, her hands still wrapped around their cocks.

"I want to try something."

She urged them closer until their knees touched her hips and brought their cocks as close together as she could working them in unison. Mac abandoned his attempt to use his mouth on her and finger fucked her instead as Willow did the same. They were all pressed so tightly together that he couldn't even see what he was doing and was grateful for the psychic feedback which showed how close Neeve was to coming for them. And it was for them. He and Willow were working perfectly together to give Neeve pleasure.

And she was working them hard…God, he wanted to climax, wanted to watch his and Willow's come explode out of their cocks, dripping down over Neeve's fingers. Even as he thought it, he got his wish and it was even better than he'd imagined it would be, even better than when Kaiden had been their third…

Willow gasped and dug his fingers into Mac's shoulder as he kept on coming, his mind enveloping Mac's and Neeve's in the enormity of his pleasure. As soon as Neeve released his cock, Mac returned to her cunt and used his fingers and his mouth to bring his female to another climax. Willow took his place and did the same thing until Neeve was screaming their names.

Willow crouched between Neeve's thighs and Mac absently stroked his hand over the other man's ass, admiring the taut muscle and the flex of his hips. Neeve finally went still and seemed to fall asleep for a moment. Mac knew it wouldn't be long before she needed them again, so he took the opportunity to go to the bathroom and wash.

Willow followed him in and used the second sink to rinse off, his green skin shining like a pearl with exertion. After he washed, Mac went hunting for some fresh towels and threw one over to his companion.

"Thank you." Willow met his gaze in the mirror. "Do you mind me being here, First Male?"

"No."

"Good." His slow smile made Mac stare hard at him. "I am honored to service you both."

Mac took the three steps that brought him across to Willow. "You don't have to serve me."

"You don't wish to fuck me?" Willow shook his head. "You are lying to yourself."

"Our job is to be here for Neeve."

"And due to our combined efforts, she is asleep now, and would not begrudge either of us the opportunity to fuck each other."

"She doesn't know—"

Willow opened his eyes wide. "That you've already touched me?" He stroked his half-hard cock. "Had you hand on my cock and your fingers in my ass?" With a sigh, he shook his head. "Of course you haven't told her. I mean nothing to you, do I?" He went to push past Mac. "I need to get back to my First Female."

"Wait." Mac put his hand on Willow's shoulder.

"For what, Ian Mac? For you to give me a chance to fully share this joining with both of you? I suspect I will be waiting a very long time for that invitation."

"For me to apologize." Mac met Willow's frustrated gaze. "I'm struggling here."

Willow's half-smiled and lowered his telepathic shields. "I'm not sure what is wrong with me, either. I never expected to get this opportunity." He shook his head. "And now I'm complaining about it not fulfilling all my fantasies when I am only here to serve and more than willing to do so."

Mac moved his hand and pinched Willow's nipple hard. "Don't undervalue yourself." His cock stirred and he was so close to the other man that he could feel Willow's excitement, too. Reaching between them he gripped Willow's cock and pressed it against his own. The bolt of pure lust that shot through them both made him almost bite his tongue.

This was way out of his comfort zone, and yet if anyone apart from Neeve had told him to stop at that moment, he would've growled at them to stand down. Touching Willow like this felt right in a way it hadn't felt even with Kaiden.

"Sit up here."

Willow braced his hands on the countertop and sat on it and Mac returned his attention to the other man's cock, rubbing it hard and watching the pre-cum at the tip gather and roll down to lubricate his fingers. The only sound was Willow's harried breathing and the slick slide of his own pumping fingers.

Adjusting his grip, Mac slid his wet thumb downward over Willow's tight balls and the soft skin of his taint. Willow moved closer to the edge of the countertop arching his hips so that Mac could reach.

"*Soap?*"

Willow leaned back and placed the dish of homemade soap by his thigh. Mac scooped up a finger full of the soft goop and circled Willow's arsehole.

"*Please, Ian Mac.*"

Mac didn't reply, his attention all on the inward plunge of his finger inside Willow's arse.

"*Gods...*"

Willow's pleasure and anticipation resonated through Mac's mind making him want to move faster, harder, to own the other man in a way that he'd never even considered owning Kaiden.

"*I am yours already, Ian Mac.*"

He glanced up from his plunging finger to find Willow staring at him, his pupils almost dilated black with lust and need.

"*I want to fuck you,*" Mac added another finger and worked Willow hard. "*I want my cock in you.*"

WITH A STIFLED SOUND, Willow brought his feet up and set them on the countertop opening himself as wide as he could to Ian Mac's fingers.

"More, give me more. Give me your cock."

He waited as Ian Mac slathered his cock in the soap and leaned forward, one hand wrapped around the base of his shaft as he sought Willow's puckered hole. Letting out his breath, he tried to relax as he was penetrated.

"God..." Ian Mac breathed hard in his mind. *"You're so tight."*

"Just fuck me, please, just—" Willow groaned out loud, the sound echoing through the bathroom as Ian Mac took him at his word and with a series of quick thrusts buried himself deep inside Willow.

Willow braced himself against Ian Mac's shoulder as the other man started to pound into him, both of their gazes directed downward toward the amazing sight of Ian Mac's cock fucking him hard.

"Hold my cock." Willow begged.

Ian Mac obliged and pumped him in time to the movement of his hips. Red hot colors flashed behind Willow's eyes and he sent the sensations out to Ian Mac and received them back. He'd never felt like this before. It was both terrifying and exhilarating at the same time. The heat between them seemed to be forming a bond, an unbreakable tie that couldn't be possible when his lover only saw him as a temporary mate to satisfy his female for three days.

A blur of movement at the door to the bathroom had Willow opening his eyes and looking over Mac's shoulder to where a naked Neeve stood watching them. When she caught his eye, she strolled over and ran a hand over Ian Mac's flexing buttock.

"Very nice, First Male. You two make a pretty picture."

To Willow's dismay, Ian Mac stopped moving. His cock was

still buried deep inside Willow but his mind slammed shut. It was like being cut off from oxygen.

"Neeve, I—"

Neeve came closer and grabbed Ian Mac's chin. "There's no need to apologize. Willow and I are Pavlovan. We understand these things, don't we, Willow?"

Willow could barely nod, the sensation of being shut out was still too painful. Neeve's expression gentled as she turned to him, and kissed him on the lips.

"You are beautiful together. Thank you for sharing yourself with him, Willow, even though he probably doesn't deserve it."

He wanted to say the right thing, the gracious thing, but for the first time in his life, the conventional words, the calmness at the center of his soul had deserted him. He could only stare into her eyes. Her gaze darkened and she slid her hand down to his cock.

"If you're done, Mac, go and shower. I'll make sure Willow is taken care of."

"I'm...not done." Ian Mac rolled his hips sending another load of sensation trembling through Willow. "Will you stay and watch?"

"I'd love to, and then we can all shower and start again." Neeve placed a hand on each of their shoulders. "I want to see you both come."

And then it was easier to simply align his mind and thoughts with his female and allow his body to take Ian Mac's cock and bring him to a fast climax. He felt the heat of his lover's come deep inside him and let himself come too, his seed pouring out over Ian Mac's fingers until he had nothing left to give.

Neeve sighed and kissed them both. "That was awesome. Now let's shower because I need some attention too."

Willow waited until Ian Mac disengaged and then slid off the countertop. His knees were shaking from being spread so wide and his ass was sore from the pounding Ian Mac had given him, but he would find the good in it. He would appreciate how much he had already been given and not yearn for more. The Oracle's prophecies could be interpreted in many different ways, so perhaps this was the best he could hope for.

He glanced over at Neeve and then more covertly at Ian Mac as they stepped into the shower. He'd already been given so much. He was a fool to have expected to have everything.

"Willow?"

Neeve beckoned to him, her smile welcoming. All Pavlovan threesomes worked differently. He would focus his attention on his female and be thankful that she at least seemed to want him unreservedly.

14

Mac woke from a hasty nap to find Willow and Neeve having sex. It was day three of her mating cycle, and she was becoming less demanding. She was straddling Willow and he was smiling up at her as she rode his cock. Luckily for Neeve, Willow's stamina was even better than Kaiden's, which meant that Mac got many opportunities to admire his two bedmates in motion. He could also sense how well their minds ran together.

Was it like that for all Pavlovans? Or was it just because he was a slightly different species that his telepathic talents were more ragged and distinct? He felt far less in control than the other two, far more eager to grab and devour each of them whole.

As if he'd spoken out loud, Willow's gaze flicked toward him.

"First Male."

"Willow."

His lover's thoughts instantly assumed another thin wall of protection. It had been like this since he'd fucked him. As if Willow either didn't want to share the bone shaking passion that had sprung up between them, or had retreated from it. Mac hadn't decided which it was yet, but it annoyed the hell out of him.

He moved behind Neeve and grabbed some lube slicking it over his hardening cock. If he couldn't fuck Willow again, he'd fuck them both, feel Neeve's arse tighten all around him and the heavy thrust of Willow's cock aligned with his in her cunt. He put his hand on the small of her back and she arched upward giving him a close view of the way Willow's big cock was spreading her pussy lips wide.

"Yeah, that's nice." He murmured as he eased inside her. "Fuck us both, First Female until you've come enough to satisfy yourself. We'll stay hard for you."

Her throaty laugh made him even hornier. "Good."

He concentrated on joining his body to hers, aware of Willow underneath her tensing as his slow penetration brought Mac's cock almost alongside his.

He nipped Neeve's throat. "Would you like us both in your cunt?"

She shuddered into a fast orgasm and he smiled against her shoulder. "I think she likes that idea, Willow."

His lover met his gaze. "It is certainly an interesting notion, Ian Mac. I tried it once and found it quite extraordinary, so with a mate it would be—" He hesitated. "I mean with your triad mates, it would be extraordinary."

There it was again, that attempt to distance himself from what was happening between the three of them. Was Willow blind? Mac sheathed himself fully in Neeve and started to work his hips back and forth pushing her down onto Willow. The feeling of both of them beneath him was incredibly powerful. He slowed down to appreciate it, and turned his thoughts inward, determined to smash through all the barriers Willow kept putting up and make him feel the same level of need and desperation he was dealing with.

Neeve climaxed and Willow's breath hissed out as she

clenched hard around him, setting Mac off into a frenzy of pumping that brought him intense relief. As he came, he reached down and fisted Willow's long hair.

"Come with me. Come for Neeve."

Willow jerked upward and started to climax, each long jet of come felt by both Mac and Neeve making Neeve climax again. Mac eased away and lifted Neeve off Willow. Holding her in his arms he took her through to the bathroom and turned the shower on.

She didn't argue with him at all, just allowed him to wash her clean, her face buried in his shoulder, her body languid and satisfied.

"Don't be mean to Willow."

He frowned as he rinsed the soap from her neck. *"Mean?"*

"Shutting him out. It's not fair. He..." she hesitated. *"He deserves more."*

"I'm not the one shutting him out. He's doing it."

"That's not what's coming through to me."

"So because you two are so in sync, it's my fault?"

She opened her eyes and blinked at him, water droplet sparkling on her eyelashes. *"Do you sense that?"*

"It's hard to miss." He turned off the water and reached for one of the towels.

"Then what's the problem?"

He gathered her up in the towel and strode back into the bedroom with her. "There isn't one. Haven't you listened to a word I've said?" His gaze fell on the empty bed. "Now where the hell has he gone?"

He dumped Neeve in the center of the bed and looked around like an idiot.

"He left a note." Neeve handed it to him. "He thanks us for the honor of being in our bed."

Mac stared at the outer door as his gut clenched in denial. He turned back to Neeve and drew an unsteady breath.

"I wasn't completely honest with you about who I messed up with on my trip. It was Willow. I touched him, I let him suck my cock."

"So?"

"I think he's *connected* to me. I'm sorry. I can't help it, Neeve. He just—" he waved his hand in a helpless gesture.

Neeve knelt up on the bed, her hands on her hips stark naked and glared at him. "Of *course* he's connected to you, you idiot. He's connected to *me*, too. He's our third."

"Our *third?*"

"Our Second Male."

"He is? Why the hell didn't anyone tell me?" Mac let out his breath. "Oh, thank God. I thought I was going crazy."

"You'd better go and find him and make things right then, hadn't you?" Neeve lay back down and pulled the covers over her. "I'm going to sleep now. Bring him back to our bed by tomorrow morning, and we'll sit down together and make this work."

Mac strode toward the door and then stopped. "I'm naked and I don't know where he's gone."

She sat up again and threw the towel at him. "Go. Think about him, and you'll find him."

He paused again at the door. "Are you sure about this?"

"Absolutely. Now go and fix this. I don't care what you have to do, but make certain he understands that we both want him *and* value him, okay?"

He wrapped the towel around his waist and saluted. "Yes, First Daughter."

Letting himself out into the long corridor that connected the suites, he paused to think about Willow and found himself being blocked by a wall of stone. It bloody hurt. Shielding his thoughts, he reached out again and concentrated on following the telepathic essence of his mate.

Ten minutes later, he walked into the guards' room, nodded

at the faces of his surprised bodyguards and pointed at the quarters beyond.

"Is Willow there?"

Ungar grinned at him. "Yes, Ian Mac."

"Thanks." He paused for a second. "Haven't you guys got anything to do?"

"Not really."

"Then block your ears, this could get noisy." He kept walking until he reached the third door on the left and knocked hard.

"Willow?"

There was no answer. He tried the handle and it opened. With a quick prayer to all the gods both Pavlovan and human, he went inside and shut the door behind him. Willow sat on the edge of his bed, his back turned to Mac. He'd obviously showered and his hair was still damp and hung freely around his shoulders.

"Why did you leave?"

Willow didn't turn around. "The First Female's mating cycle had finished. I was no longer required."

"So you just walked away."

"I...thought to make our parting less awkward." His shoulder hunched. "I did not wish to embarrass either of you."

Mac crossed the room and crouched down in front of Willow who was staring pensively at the floor, his long fair hair shielding his face. He finally raised his head and smiled at Mac.

"I will never forget you both. You gave me the most astounding gift a male could ever wish for."

"Bullshit."

Willow blinked at him. "I beg your pardon?"

"That's enough for you, is it? Truthfully?" He put his hands on Willow's knees and pushed them wide. "Don't you want more? My mouth on your dick, your cock buried deep in my arse..."

Willow shuddered as Mac took a deep breath and leaned in to lick his lover's already thickening shaft. "I want to suck you."

"What good will it do?" Willow asked. "Do you want me to feel even worse about what I'm about to lose?"

"Who says you're going to lose? When we've finished this, we're both going back to Neeve's bed. She has a few things she wants to say to you." Mac slid his tongue into the wet slit of Willow's straining cock. "I prefer to give you a practical demonstration of how I feel right here on my knees while I get you hard enough to fuck me."

"You don't have to do this, Ian Mac."

Mac raised his head. "Yes I damn well do. How else are you going to understand that I can't function without you and Neeve in my life?"

"*Both* of us?"

"That's how a triad usually works, isn't it?"

"You accept me as your third?"

"After Neeve slapped me around the head and pointed it out to me—yes."

Willow swallowed hard and his gaze softened. "Gods, Ian Mac, I—"

"No more talking. I want to taste you."

Mac slowly sucked Willow's cock into his mouth and then took even more. Willow's hand slid into his hair to cup his skull as Mac began to slide his mouth up and down his lover's hot pulsing flesh. He closed his eyes to concentrate, letting Willow's emotions guide him into giving pleasure and not thinking about the fact that he'd never have dreamed he'd be so eager to suck another man's dick.

"Esca was right. When it's the right person attached to the cock one is required to suck, it suddenly makes perfect sense."

Willow's amusement flooded through him, and he focused even harder, until his companion stopped being careful and started to fuck his mouth with each thrust of his hips, his hand holding Mac's head just where he wanted him.

And Mac took it all. Took Willow's cock until he flooded his throat with come. When Willow finished shuddering, Mac climbed up on the bed and drew the other man down beside him, chest to chest, knee to knee, face to face. A strange sensation of peace stole over him and he knew it emanated from Willow. They might be opposites, but they complemented each other in ways that astounded him.

Willow touched his face. "I dreamed of this, Ian Mac. Lying here with you." He hesitated. "When I thought you didn't want me, I believed the Oracle had deceived me. For the first time in my life, I doubted myself and all my certainties."

"The Oracle told you about me?"

He nodded. "When I reached the age of eighteen years and went to the temple complex to be received as an adult. She said I would have to wait as many years as I already had for my mates to arrive. When I saw you…I knew you were the one, and then I met Neeve and I was certain."

"So was Neeve. It was only the idiot from Earth who didn't get it."

Willow smiled at him. "You have worked it out now, First Male." His expression became more serious. "You do not have to let me fuck you, Ian Mac. Not all triads are equal."

"That's good to know but, hell…" Mac gathered his courage and looked right into Willow's silver eyes. "Every time you had Neeve like that, I wondered how it would feel, how you would fit inside me."

Willow glanced down at his cock. "I'm big."

"I noticed that." Mac licked his lips. "I've already had you crammed down my throat."

"I'd be careful."

Mac nodded, his gaze riveted on Willow's smiling mouth. "Then I'm yours."

"Then lie back and let me take what is mine." Willow whispered.

Ian Mac rolled over onto his back and Willow undid the towel wrapped around his lover's waist and threw it onto the floor. With careful hands, he traced his fingers down over Ian Mac's arms and then his chest, narrow waist and lean hips. His mate was beautiful. Taller than Willow, but no less muscular. When they were better acquainted in bed, it would be a pleasure to measure his strength against this man's…

"Fighting *and* fucking." Ian Mac murmured. "I look forward to that."

Willow kissed and licked Ian Mac's nipple and then drew it into his mouth to suck until his lover was writhing against the sheets. His cock pressing urgently against Willow's stomach leaving trails of glistening pre-cum that connected their bodies.

With a grateful sigh, Willow kissed and licked his way over Ian Mac's chest, following the line of dark hair down to his groin, and then diverting to his hips and thighs.

"Touch my cock."

The telepathic plea was urgent. Willow smiled as he bit the inside of Ian Mac's thigh.

"Not yet."

"Please."

"But I am enjoying making you pay for not realizing I was your mate, Ian Mac."

His lover shifted restlessly on the sheets. *"Then I suppose I'll have to bear it."*

Willow gently ran his tongue over Ian Mac's balls and the underside of his cock, making him hiss out a curse. He licked up the pre-cum that ran down Ian Mac's shaft savoring the taste and then rose over him to press his mouth to his mate's. With a groan, Ian Mac let him in, battling with Willow and sucking his own essence off Willow's thrusting tongue.

"Do you like your taste, my mate? Do you know how it drives me wild knowing I made you this wet even after three days of serving our Female?"

Willow released Ian Mac's mouth and kissed his way down to his cock again, this time taking it carefully in his mouth while his fingers stroked lower, cupping his balls and stroking backward across the smooth skin of his taint to his lover's tight ass hole.

"God..."

Without taking his mouth away from Ian Mac's cock, Willow reached out a hand and yanked open the drawer beside his bed, his fingers seeking the unscented oil he kept there.

"I take it I'm not the first man you've fucked, Willow?"

"Not the first. But definitely the last."

"Good to know."

"I'll make this good for you, Ian Mac, I swear it."

He felt his lover's hand touch his hair. *"Because I've never done this before."*

"Taken a man inside you?" Willow went still. *"Then I am doubly honored and humbled by your trust in me, First Male."*

"And I wish you would stop being so fucking formal and get on with it." Willow snorted and Ian Mac's grip on his hair tightened. *"Please."*

"As you wish, First Male."

Willow eased the tip of his well-lubed finger inside Ian Mac and felt his helpless shudder of response. As he pushed deeper, he sucked carefully at his lover's cock, keeping his hips moving, keeping him aroused and willing to take more with each subtle push of his finger. Soon it became easier and he added another finger, widening Ian Mac for the invasion to come, and then added a third. Increasing the pressure of his sucking on Ian

Mac's cock, he kept his mate occupied with the influx of constant pleasure while he readied his own cock.

Even so, he hesitated when he looked down at his eager cock and considered how tight Ian Mac was going to be. Hard fingers wove into his hair and his lover pulled his head down.

"Just do it, Willow. I don't care if it hurts. I just want you inside me."

"If you insist."

Willow wrapped his fingers around the base of his shaft and introduced the tip to the well-oiled ring of muscle around Ian Mac's entrance. He held his breath as he was able to move inward, aware of the silence in his mate's head and of every nuance of his anticipation.

"Relax for me, Ian Mac," he murmured.

"That's damned hard to do when you are so...*goddam it...* fucking *huge*." Ian Mac said through clenched teeth.

Willow claimed his mouth and his cock using his fingers and tongue to distract Ian Mac as he slowly and carefully pushed deeper. Gods, he wanted to come himself, the tight grip on his cock was intoxicating. He took a deep calming breath and opened his mind to Ian Mac, sharing his experience. His lover angled his hips allowing him deeper, his mind now flowing in tune with Willow's. Every inch gained, every thrill of pleasure, was shared between them in an endless erotic cycle. Discomfort was forgotten in the urgent need to possess the other, to share such an unforgettable moment...

Willow slowly opened his eyes and looked down at Ian Mac who was staring right back at him, his blue eyes narrowed with lust, his muscular frame pinned to the bed with the weight of Willow's body over him.

"May I move now?" Willow asked.

"I'll probably come if you do. I'm barely holding it together as it is."

"You won't come, Ian Mac. You'll wait for me." Holding his

lover's gaze, Willow began to move very gently back and forth until he had to shut his eyes against the glorious bloom of lust and desire in Ian Mac's face.

"God—that's—" His lover clutched Willow's arm and held on, his grip ferocious. Not that Willow cared, he was too far gone to do anything but thrust his hips and forge his way to a climax that would bring him and Ian Mac to a new level of bonding he'd never experienced with another male.

Reaching down, he reclaimed Ian Mac's cock and pumped it hard in time to his own thrusts. *"Come with me, come together."*

Inside his head, Ian Mac roared as he started to come, setting Willow off, too, and then there was nothing but pure sensation and the swirling entity of him and his mate that contained both their souls and would never let them be completely apart again.

He fell forward over Ian Mac, catching himself on his hands and tried to remember how to breathe. His lover wrapped an arm around his shoulders and held him in place as they both tried to reassemble their sense of self and disengage both physically and mentally.

After a long while, when their breathing had returned to normal, Ian Mac croaked. "Shower."

And Willow rolled off him and onto his feet. His whole body was trembling.

He led the way into the small bathroom and turned on the shower. It was a squeeze to fit them both in the stall, but they managed it, mainly because they didn't mind washing any bits of the other if they got confused. Washing turned to other interesting things, and Willow ended up wet and naked and on all fours on the bed being fucked from behind.

Not that he minded having another shower at all…

After they'd both dried off and returned to make the disordered bed so they could sleep in it, Willow went down on his knees in front of Ian Mac.

"First Male." He reached for Ian Mac's hand and kissed his fingers.

"You're getting formal again."

Willow looked up at him. "It is simply a matter of respect and acknowledgement of our relative positions within the triad."

"Then what am I required to do in return?"

"Put your hand on the top of my head and acknowledge me by saying, 'Second Male.'"

"But we already know these things. And, I don't believe you are inferior to me—"

Willow remained kneeling. "Ian Mac." He said politely, but firmly. "It would mean a great deal to me if you would do this."

He heard his lover sigh as his hand touched Willow's hair.

"Second Male."

"First."

Willow rose and smiled into his Ian Mac's perturbed face. "Thank you."

"I'll do it for you, but it doesn't mean anything, okay?"

"It means the world to me."

Ian Mac grinned. "Then you're as crazy as I am. Let's go to sleep and take ourselves back to Neeve in the morning as ordered." He yawned so hard he cracked his jaw. "We probably woke her up with all that sex anyway."

"You did. And I can't wait to experience it at first hand in the morning."

Willow smiled as the voice of their First Female resonated through both their minds.

"We will return to you at first light, First Female."

"Make it lunchtime and I might be awake."

Willow climbed into bed and Ian Mac followed him. And for the first time in his life, despite having everything in the universe to be thankful for, Willow forgot to say his prayers and fell fast asleep.

15

"Neeve?"

Neeve opened her eyes to find her mother standing by her bed. It was still dark and she was wearing her nightgown.

"What's up?"

Her mother shuddered. "That is a very unfortunate way of a conversing that you picked up from Ian, daughter. I don't like it."

Neeve sat up, aware that she was naked and that her bed looked and smelled like there had recently been three highly sexed adults romping on it—which there had been.

"How can I help you, Mother, dear?"

"I need you to come to the temple."

"Why?"

"Something is amiss."

"With what?"

"I'm not sure. That's why I need to consult the Gods."

Neeve cast a look outside at the bruised purple skies. "Right now?"

Gisele grabbed her hand. "Please, I wouldn't ask, but this is important. I sense danger among us."

"Then let me get hold of Mac and Willow. They can come, too."

Grumbling under her breath but seriously worried by her mother's urgency, Neeve got out of bed, pulled on a pair of running shorts and a T-shirt that belonged to Mac. She also took his gun from his holster and stuck it into the back pocket of her shorts concealing it under the T-shirt. Her mother didn't approve of weapons, but Neeve had learned to be careful on Earth.

"Okay, let's go."

She followed her mother out onto the balcony where Ungar fell in behind them like a silent green shadow. They used the quickest and most private route to approach the inner sanctum of the temple. As they climbed the marble steps, Neeve also looked around her, aware that something wasn't right, that *something* was disrupting the peace and power of the place. Her mother reached back to grab her hand and their telepathic connection strengthened her.

"*There is someone in the inner sanctum.*"

"*What?*"

Before Neeve's eyes, Gisele disappeared and was replaced by the majesty of the Oracle in an awesomely foul mood. "*How dare someone desecrate my temple!*"

Ungar stepped in front of them both. "*Let me go first.*"

The pure white light that normally surrounded the sanctuary where her mother's ancient throne and the source of the sacred spring resided was bathed in flickering red and orange flames.

"*No!*" The Oracle's voice boomed out physically and telepathically. Neeve wanted to cover her ears at the power as her mother started to run toward the sanctuary.

"*Mother, don't!*" She grabbed for the Oracle's sleeve, but missed and had to increase her speed. Heat built in front of her and she started to cough.

"Stop! It might be a trap!"

Even as her mother half-turned back, several figures appeared from behind the pillars and converged on them. Something hit Neeve on the back of the head and she was engulfed in blackness. She cried out for her mates, a cry she couldn't control and the last sound she was allowed to make before blackness enfolded her.

MAC SAT bolt upright in the bed, only to see that Willow was already standing beside it.

"What the fuck just happened to Neeve? She screamed our names and now I can't feel her anymore."

"She and the Oracle are in trouble. We must go, *now.*"

Even as he spoke, Willow was grabbing his bow and arrow and a variety of daggers. Mac got up too and realized all he had to put on was a towel.

Willow glanced up from his preparations. "Clothes in my chest on the floor, weapons I will give you as we proceed."

Mac grabbed a pair of soft buckskin pants and a white shirt and ran after his mate. "How are we supposed to find them? I can't *feel* her."

Willow pointed up at the temple, which was on fire. "I suggest we start there."

"Holy fuck, what happened?"

Willow didn't bother to answer him as they made their way as stealthily as they could through the narrow passages known only to the bodyguards that led to the summit. People were converging on the temple from all sides now. Mac suddenly stopped and grabbed Willow's arm.

"They're not going to be up there."

"But they might be trapped inside."

"No. If they are in there, they're dead, or someone will get them out much faster than we can reach them. It's far more likely they've been taken somewhere else. Come on."

He ran to the edge of the steep pathway where he had an overview of the whole complex and engaged his biometric tracking skills. A grid of the temple unfolded in his head and he surveyed the area. Data ticked through his consciousness of what was usual, and what was out of place.

"Give me your power."

Willow added his telepathic strength to Mac's and the data stream speeded up.

Mac pointed at a group of trees behind the temple.

"Up there against the cliff. There's some kind of craft. I can read an energy stream."

He started running, and Willow followed without hesitation. They passed through one of the security gates where Mac was able to pick up a weapon. Willow updated the Hakron tribe as they ran. If anyone knew how to track the Oracle and her daughter in the jungle it would be them.

Mac glanced back at Willow who was looking as grim-faced as he was.

"Can you sense the Oracle?"

"Yes, she is of our blood."

"And Neeve?"

"She isn't dead, First Male. You'd know if she was. It would feel as if your soul was being ripped apart." He pushed past Mac. *"Let me lead, I know the terrain better and can get us to the place faster."*

Mac didn't argue with that. He had a terrible sense that time was running out. If the shuttle took off, the Pavlovan nation would lose its Oracle and her heir. He followed Willow in single file, using his mate's footsteps as a guide and moving as quietly as he could through the uphill terrain. They came to the edge of a clearing where a small six-man shuttle had been set down. There were no identifying marks on the craft, or any sign of activity.

Willow went down on one knee behind the tall scrubby foliage and Mac did the same.

"I don't see any movement."

"They are in hostile territory. It is also possible that we have reached this place ahead of our prey." Willow pointed to the other side of the clearing. *"Something is coming."*

The faint sense of another telepathic signal searching the area made Mac raise his shields. He felt Willow do the same.

"Etruscan telepath."

Their mating link meant they could still communicate despite blocking everyone else out.

"Damn, how the hell did they land here without being detected?" If he survived the present crisis, Mac intended to have a serious conversation with the Pavlovan military about their security network.

"I have no idea. How many are you picking up?"

"Six, you?"

The same, including the telepath who is the only female. They probably thought to have the element of surprise, not realizing the First Daughter has her two bonded males with her."

"Agreed." Mac tensed. How the hell could they have left Neeve alone? He'd never forgive himself if she were hurt. *"Here they come."*

NEEVE OPENED ONE EYE, aware that something wasn't right and that her world was inverted and bumpy and basically painful. The grunt of someone breathing heavily against her ear made her try to turn her head. They were moving through the jungle and away from the temple. She was being carried over someone's shoulder, as was her mother.

There was another telepath present, a small fair woman who jogged alongside the much bigger soldiers. Not wanting the female to know she was conscious, Neeve tried to tighten her shields, which made her head hurt even more.

"We're here."

The voice of the man who was carrying her was low-pitched but distinct enough for Neeve to detect an Etruscan accent.

"Put them down close to the ship."

The rumbling voice continued. "Pazz and Tetra stand guard. If they move shoot them dead."

Her world tipped crazily again as she was lowered unceremoniously onto the ground next to the still body of her mother.

"*Shoot* them, sir?" The female said. "I thought our orders were to—"

"No one gives a freck what you think, telepath, so shut it, and obey orders or I'll shoot *you* for insubordination."

"Yes, sir."

The rest of the men, Neeve counted four of them went aboard the shuttle. Within seconds, a low hum of power emanated from the engines blowing hot puffs of air across Neeve's skin.

"*First Female.*" The whisper of a thought from Willow made Neeve want to shout out in triumph. "*Protect your mother.*"

Neeve tensed as the female soldier turned toward the shuttle. "Sir? I think—"

"Frecking hell, Tetra!" The commander came out of the shuttle and headed straight for them. "You got a death wish or something? I told you not to disturb me."

"But—" There was a gasp and the telepath ended up curled on the ground next to Neeve, her mouth bleeding.

The Etruscan laughed and aimed a kick at the female's ribs before turning his attention to Neeve's mother. He crouched down beside the Oracle and touched her hair.

"She looks pretty good for a two hundred year old goddess. Quite fuckable, in fact. If we hadn't been given our orders. I'd take her back with us and try her on for size."

Rage blistered through Neeve's entire body. She wasn't aware of standing up only that she was pointing her finger at the Etruscan commander. A voice she didn't recognize roared out of her.

"Do not touch the Oracle!"

"Yeah, right, sweetheart. Now shut the freck up."

The commander grinned and pointed his weapon at her. Neeve closed her eyes and let the power of her rage consume her. There was a booming sound and then a crackle of burning flesh. Someone tackled her from behind, picked her up and ran. She started to struggle and then realized it was Mac.

"Let me go!" She shouted through the noise. "My mother!"

"Willow has her." Mac's hand tightened in her hair. "It's okay, don't look back, it's going to be okay."

She wrenched herself out of his hold and turned to look at the clearing. It looked like someone had dropped a bomb on it. The shuttle was a charred, blackened shell, and the people… there were no people. She swallowed hard as she registered the small piles of ashes.

"Did I do that? Holy *meershit*."

"Yeah." Mac touched her shoulder. "Remind me never to piss you off."

"I…" she shook her head. "I didn't mean it to happen. That man touched my mother, he was threatening to rape her…" She shivered and Mac put his arm around her shoulder.

"Whatever you did, Neeve, it was totally justified. You saved yourself and your mother." He paused. "Willow and I were just about to rush to your aid, but you did a much better job of it."

"I'm a *monster*."

He put his hand under her chin and made her look up at him. "No you're not. You're the Oracle's First Daughter. You might not want to be that person, but you sure as hell are capable of amazing things." He hesitated for a second. "How long do Oracles live, give or take a hundred years?"

"About five hundred."

"So, if you do decide to embrace your powers, you've still got a couple of hundred years to get used to the idea, right?"

She nodded as his solemn face went all blurry.

"Don't cry."

She nodded again as her tears continued to fall.

"*Neeve.*"

She turned to find her mother looking up at her and went down on her knees. "Oracle."

"You saved my life, First Daughter. You came into your true powers with your triad." Her mother's voice wobbled. "Thank you."

Neeve kissed the Oracle's hand. "You are welcome, Mom."

"Now I just need to teach you how to *control* your powers."

Neeve stood up and managed a shaky grin. "You mean I don't have to annihilate everyone all the time? I think Mac and Willow will be pleased to hear that."

"You will learn, Neeve. I will show you. It will be a great honor."

She squeezed her mother's fingers. "I know."

After taking another deep breath, she turned to Willow, who was smiling at her.

"Where's the Etruscan telepath?"

"She had the sense to run into the jungle the moment you stood up. I've sent Ungar to find her and bring her back to the temple."

"Good. She doesn't deserve to suffer for what happened. She tried to protect us."

"So I saw. I suspect if she wants to stay she will find her talents far more welcome here than in Etrusca." Willow stepped in and kissed her cheek. "I am most proud of you. First Daughter. You saved the Oracle."

"Just the Oracle?"

She met his silver gaze, which was full of love and respect. Mac joined them and for a precious moment, they both took her hands. Power rose and surged between them blending into something new and unique that contained them all, but was even greater than the sum of its parts.

"And yourself," Willow murmured. "And us. We are yours, First Female for as long as you live."

"Which by the sound of it could be a bloody long time." Mac said. "She'll have worn us both out by the time we turn fifty."

"Don't you remember?" Neeve shook her head. "The triad shares everything, Ian McNeill. You're going to have to put up with me for a lot longer than that."

The expression on his face almost made her want to kiss him. But that would come later. Much later after they'd alerted the assembly, contacted Ash, reviewed security and made sure her mother was all right.

But it would happen.

Much like her destiny.

Heeze, was she finally growing up? She took a deep breath and went over to her mother. "We'll leave these two here to deal with this mess, and I'll take you to the healers. Willow says the damage to the inner sanctum is minimal. It was just to draw us into their trap."

"Good," her mother pressed a hand to her head and winced. "I'm feeling rather strange."

Neeve linked her arm through her mother's offering her support." Do you think you can make it? We can't fly can we? That would be an awesome super power."

"I've never tried." Her mother's soft laughter flowed through Neeve. "I'm quite capable of walking back to the temple with you."

"Good." Neeve replied. "Being able to incinerate people with a flick of my fingers is quite enough to deal with for one day."

"Neeve."

She only stopped walking because her mother had.

"Stop being flippant and trying to pretend that didn't frighten you."

"Frighten me? It *terrified* me." She shuddered. "What if I had a row with Mac and I accidentally fried him?"

"You wouldn't do that."

"I don't know, he can be damned annoying sometimes."

"*Neeve.*" The Oracle touched her cheek. "It's all right. I'll teach you how to manage your powers. Now that you have accepted that you have them, you will learn quickly."

"I hope so." She frowned. "Even though that man deserved to die for touching you, the other's didn't."

"I read their thoughts. Neeve." Her mother's eyes hardened. "They all knew the purpose of their mission. They had been sent to kill us. They were all guilty apart from that poor empath. If you hadn't acted, the Pavlovan nation would've been left without the two key figures of their belief system—you and me."

"That would've been terrible."

"Yes. Being the Oracle brings great power, but that power is placed at the service of the nation. You preserved that. You did the right thing."

"That's what Mac and Willow said, too."

"Then we are all in agreement. Now, come on, it is getting rather cold out here."

"Yes, Gisele."

After one more deep breath, Neeve turned away from the scene of the disaster and followed her mother up to the temple. So, one day she was going to be the Oracle of Pavlovan.

One day she might even be okay with that.

Her mother took her hand, and together they ascended the steps, acknowledging the relief and joy of the crowds. Neeve had another thought.

With Mac and Willow at her side, *heeze*, she might even enjoy it…

The End

209

NOTE FOR READERS

Dear Reader,

I hope you enjoyed the second installment of my science fiction erotic romance series Triad. I enjoy writing these books and already have the next one written and ready for you.

If you enjoy the books, please consider reviewing them. I love to hear what readers think about my characters.

If you want to read more of my books, please check out my website and consider joining my newsletter for the fastest updates and early contests to win new books.

katepearce.com/newsletter

Thank you for reading!
Kate Pearce

Prologue

York, England 970. A.D.

"We're not going to survive this time, brother." Aki's voice echoed around the dark cavern as they ran. "Someone betrayed us."

"I know that," Einarr snarled. "And, by the Gods, he will regret it."

"If we live."

Einarr took another turn and continued downward, the sound of underground water now in front of him. "We'll live." He slowed his step, as the light ahead grew stronger.

"By running away like cowards?" Aki was breathing hard. "They've blocked the entrance to this cave. All they have to do is come after us. We'll be easy prey."

"We're not running away." The eerie white light bounced off Einarr's shield and axe. The power of his ancestors surged within him and answered the call of the ancient magic. "Grandfather told me about this place. He said that if I ever needed an escape, the waterfall would provide one."

Aki gasped as they stepped into a huge cavern where water tumbled in a frothing white mass down from the farthest black rock formation.

"There's a way out?" Aki had to yell to be heard.

Einarr reached behind him and grasped Aki's arm ring, sending a wave of power that pushed his words directly into his twin brother's head.

"Aye. Behind the waterfall. We just have to walk through to the other side." Einarr took a step forward, one hand on his axe. *"Be careful. It's slippery."*

Aki followed him as the well-worn path climbed steadily until they reached a smooth stone platform that seemed to disappear directly inside the roar of the white-flecked water. Einarr set down his shield and his brother did the same.

"Hold onto my cloak." Einarr said.

"I'm not a babe in arms," Aki complained, but obeyed him anyway. "May Odin protect us."

As Einarr inched forward, everything inside him slowed and coalesced into a burning hot sensation in his fingertips. He reached out his hand and the water turned to steam, lifting the curtain to show him the continuing path and a narrow cavern behind the falls. He kept moving and the waterfall closed behind them leaving an eerie screaming silence that made him want to shove his fingers in his ears and shriek like a frightened child.

The noise rose until the rocks were vibrating, and all the hair on his body stood upright like an animal at bay. Sparks flew from his outstretched fingertips ricocheting off the walls and slicing through the water like the sharpest dagger cuts.

"Einarr!"

He looked back and Aki screamed as the water turned inward and coalesced into ice. Then he knew no more.

End of Sample

To continue reading, be sure to pick up Viking Unbound at your favorite retailer.

The Sinners Club

Historical Erotic Romance

When intrigue collides with heated passion behind the closed doors of the Sinners Club there is nowhere left to hide.

.

The Morgan Ranch Series

Contemporary Western Romance

A Northern Californian ranching family torn apart by tragedy reluctantly return home to discover not everything was as they thought it was, and that love, and forgiveness can sometimes go hand in hand.

.

The Millers of Morgan Valley Series

Contemporary Western Romance

When the mother you haven't seen for twenty years asks to visit your family ranch and set the record straight, how will her ex and six adult children react? The loves and sometimes messy lives of a ranching family.

.

The Turner Brothers

Contemporary Erotic Western Romance

Three half-brothers find their own uniquely passionate ways to find the loves of their lives and accept exactly who they are—no holds barred.

.

The Obsidian Series

Sci-Fi Romance

Join a renegade band of telepaths roaming the galaxy to protect and rescue their race from the evil empire intent on destroying them.

·

Planet Valhalla Series

Sci-Fi/Futuristic Erotic Romance

One human female crash lands on a planet full of men descended from the Vikings, one of whom is the King who claims her as his mate— what could possibly go wrong? A sexy romp through the stars with excessive sex, a touch of humor and some very satisfied women…

·

The Triad Series

Sci-Fi/Futuristic Erotic Romance

Welcome to an imaginary world where civilizations, clash against the new and unknown, where telepaths are revered and reviled, and where your destiny can be preordained by a living oracle. Add in a group of super-soldier telepaths rescued from Earth and forming sexual triads for life becomes even more complex and life changing.

·

The Tribute Series

Sci-Fi/Futuristic *Dark* Erotic Romance

To save their planet from extinction the government will demand everything from the condemned few—willingly or not.

"Fans of no-holds-barred erotic portrayals of non- and quasi-consensual encounters will devour this steamy triptych."

– Publishers Weekly

·

Soul Justice Series

Paranormal Romance

Come and join a San Francisco based secret government department who investigate the monsters under the bed while risking their psychic abilities and even their own lives.

·

The Tudor Vampire Chronicles

Paranormal Historical Romance

Druids, Vampires and the court of King Henry VIII and his many wives form the backbone of this intriguing series as good fights evil through the first ever female Vampire slayer of her line, Rosalind Llewellyn.

·

Kurland St. Mary Mysteries

Historical Mystery

Writing as Catherine Lloyd

Join wounded cavalry hero Major Sir Robert Kurland and Lucy Harrington the rector's eldest daughter as they solve crimes in their quiet little village and gradually learn to appreciate each other.

ABOUT KATE PEARCE

New York Times and *USA Today* bestselling author Kate Pearce was born in England in the middle of a large family of girls and quickly found that her imagination was far more interesting than real life. After acquiring a degree in history and barely escaping from the British Civil Service alive, she moved to California and then to Hawaii with her kids and her husband and set about reinventing herself as a romance writer.

She is known for both her unconventional heroes and her joy at subverting romance clichés. In her spare time she self publishes science fiction erotic romance, historical romance, and whatever else she can imagine. You can find Kate at katepearce.com.

amazon.com/author/katepearce
goodreads.com/katepearce
bookbub.com/authors/kate-pearce
facebook.com/KatePearceAuthor
twitter.com/kate4queen